KING PENGUIN

HEARTS OF GOLD

Clive Sinclair was born in 1948 and educated at the universities of East Anglia and California at Santa Cruz. His stories, interviews and travel pieces have been published in *Encounter*, *The Year's Best Horror Stories*, *New Review*, *London Magazine*, *Penthouse*, *Club International*, *Transatlantic Review*, *Lillit* and *Monat*. His first novel, *Bibliosexuality*, was published in 1973, and he is currently writing a book about the authors, Isaac Bashevis Singer and his brother I. J. Singer. He was awarded the Bicentennial Arts Fellowship for 1980, and won the Somerset Maugham Award for 1981 with *Hearts of Gold*.

David Gamper

CLIVE SINCLAIR

HEARTS OF GOLD

A KING PENGUIN

PUBLISHED BY PENGUIN BOOKS

Penguin Books Ltd, Harmondsworth, Middlesex, England
Penguin Books, 625 Madison Avenue, New York, New York 10022, U.S.A.
Penguin Books Australia Ltd, Ringwood, Victoria, Australia
Penguin Books Canada Ltd, 2801 John Street, Markham, Ontario, Canada L3R 1B4
Penguin Books (N.Z.) Ltd, 182-190 Wairau Road, Auckland 10, New Zealand

—

First published by Allison and Busby Ltd 1979
Published in Penguin Books 1982

—

Copyright © Clive Sinclair, 1979
All rights reserved

—

Made and printed in Great Britain by
Hazell Watson & Viney Ltd, Aylesbury, Bucks
Set in Lectura

CONTENTS

Acknowledgements are due to the following publications where some of these stories first appeared:
Encounter ("A Moment of Happiness", "The Luftmensh"), *Transatlantic Review* ("Uncle Vlad"), *Club International* ("A French Letter", now entitled "Tante Rouge"), *Penthouse* ("Trial by Ordeal", now entitled "Le Docteur Enchaîné"), *London Magazine* ("The Creature on My Back").

The lines on page 30 are from "A Song About Rest" by Yehuda Amichai, and translated by Ted Hughes; the poem was published in *Amen*, Oxford University Press, 1978.

The lines on page 52 are from "I Should Have Died With You" by Halper Leivick; the poem is included in *An Anthology of Modern Yiddish Literature*, ed. Joseph Leftwich, The Hague, 1974.
The lines on page 57 originally appeared in *Black Power*, June 1967.

FOR FRAN

UNCLE VLAD

A small puff of powder cleared and I saw my aunt touch my uncle on his white cheek with such exquisite precision that she left lip marks like the wings of a ruby butterfly. I watched her for nine times nine swings of the golden pendulum as she walked from guest to guest leaving behind trails of the silver dust that sparkled in the lamplight. It was as though the entire effort of her toilet was not so much designed to establish a character as to create an impression that would leave a colourful insignia on the memory. Her voice floated on her breath, a soft wind that bent and bared the necks of her listeners before her; I heard her whisper imaginary family secrets to an English aesthete who made notes behind her back:

"I believe that Lupus thinks that Vlad married me on purely scientific principles as the best specimen he could find of a modern butterfly."

The aesthete laughed. "Well, Countess," he said, "I hope he won't stick pins into you."

Then they both swirled away in a creamy whirl of silk out into the milky way of moonlight and left behind the delicate blooms and rouged cheeks. Uncle Vlad smiled at my aunt's joke and followed her silhouette as it flitted among the lace curtains, but he remained where he was, still standing beneath the candelabra, wax dripping on to his white hair, holding several glass jars, some containing ether, others containing frantic beating moths, one containing champagne.

Our family is old and distinguished, descended from the ancient mountain lords down into a lowland mansion. Uncle Vlad, tall and grand, the head of the house, is himself called after our most famous ancestor Vled the Impaler, who finally drove the Turks from Europe, so named because of his sanguine habit of tossing Turkish captives into the air and catching them on the point of a spear. We have a portrait in the Great Hall of Vled standing in a full field of flowers amid the dying Turks who, pierced through the middle, and waving their arms and legs, look like a multitude of ecstatic butterflies. Beneath this scene in now smoked grey this legend is painted in Roman print — *Vled I called The Impaler*. "Vlad" is the modern corruption of the venerable Vled, the result of an obscure etymological whim. However, there is no disguising the physical similarities; it is all but impossible to detect a difference between the painting of Vled and the face of Uncle Vlad. Uncle Vlad is an honoured lepidopterist, but, as a rule, does not sail about honey fields in short trousers; instead he goes out at night and gathers moths by candlelight. He exchanges these easily, because of his skill and their unique paleness, for the more brightly coloured varieties, which he mounts, simply, by driving a needle through their bodies. Uncle Vlad's pursuit is looked upon with much interest by the distant Viennese branch of our family which maintains, to a doctor, that it is a genuine genetic manifestation of his more barbaric prototype; while another more émigré branch claims that Uncle Vlad is a veritable paragon of the pattern of behaviourism in that, having seen the painting of Vled at an early age, he has ever since sought to realise the contents within the limitations of his own civilised environment. Uncle Vlad believes greatly in tradition.

Every year, on a fixed day, the entire family gathers at our home to celebrate the generations with a gorgeous extravagance. My uncle and aunt occupy weeks in anticipation of the fantastic evening, working and reworking menus, always seeking a sublime gastronomic equilibrium, so that the discards look like nothing more than the drafts of meticulous lyric poems. And what poets they are! Garbure Béarnaise, Truites au Bleu, Grives au Genièvre, Canard au Sang, Crêpes Flambés aux Papillons. They strive to astonish the most sophisticated taste, the only applause they seek is the thick sound of the satisfied tongue clapping the palatine papillae. Once Uncle Vlad said to my aunt, at the supreme moment before the food is collected, "Should we not share the secrets of our art with the swine that starve?" And she replied, "Let them eat words."

Our family is proud and jealous of its dark arboreal rebus.

This year, being the first congregation since my coming of age, I was permitted to help in the preparations. On the eve, I went out alone into the nocturnal wood, carrying my rods and nets, and followed the overgrown path to the gilt river. And there I sat in silence for many hours until my nets were full, very content, for there are few sights more beautiful than that of the silver fish struggling in the moonlight. I left the fish where they were, because it was vital to keep them alive, and commenced the journey back, proud that I had completed my task so well. But I had gone no more than a kilometer towards the residence when I heard a rustling of dead leaves and the final cry of a bird in pain. I pushed my way through the bushes in the direction of the sound and came into the perfect circle of a moonbright glade. The air was full of the melodious song of a score or more of thrushes. The birds were all on the ground, trapped in Uncle Vlad's subtle snares, and they did not look real but seemed to be some eccentric ornament of the night.

Uncle Vlad himself, dressed by the shadows as a harlequin, was stepping among the thrushes and killing them one by one by gently pressing their soft necks between his thumb and forefinger. Each death, save for the single scream and the frightened flap of the wings, was conducted in complete silence: until the survivors sang again. Uncle Vlad saw me and allowed me to help.

"My boy," he whispered to me as we worked, "how was the fishing?"

"It was good, Uncle," I replied, "I caught twenty trout."

When we had finished Uncle Vlad collected all the tight bodies into a little bundle and opened a sack of the finest silk. But before he dropped the birds into it he bit off their heads. Fine tributaries of blood ran from his swelling lips.

"The thrushes always come to this spot," he said, "they cannot resist my special snails."

The kitchen was already full with the shadowy figures of our servants when we returned, and my aunt was throwing resinous logs into the dancing flames. One of the anonymous cooks was apparent through a vaporous curtain of steam, stirring a dull copper soup-pot bubbling with boiling water and vegetables.

"There must be no garlic in the Garbure Béarnaise!" Uncle
Vlad called out as we entered.

"Of course not, my dear," replied my aunt. "Did you do well?"

Uncle Vlad emptied his bag out on to the ancient wooden table,
and at once long fingers fluttered out of the obscurity and plucked
the feathers from the bodies. Then the birds were split open with
sharp knives and stuffed till they were full with peppercorn and
juniper. When this was done to the satisfaction of my uncle the
breasts were sewn up, and the birds wrapped in slices of pork lard,
and bound, ready to be cooked.

"We shall eat well tomorrow," said my aunt to me.

Exactly one hour before we were due to dine, when all our guests
were safely arrived, we killed the ducks. We took seven regal
mallards from the lake and suffocated them by wringing their
necks and pressing their breasts. The carcasses were given to the
cooks, under the supervision of my aunt, to dress and draw, while
Uncle Vlad and I went out with a large tank to collect the patient
trout. And when we carried it back into the kitchen the oval tank
seemed to have a shining lid, so full was it with fish. The remains
of the ducks were ready in the great meat press waiting only for
my uncle to add his libation of red wine. Then the press was
turned and the blood and wine was caught as it ran, by Uncle
Vlad, in goblets of gold and poured into a silver bowl. Pure vinegar
was heated in large pans, over the oven, until it boiled.

"Throw in the fish while they still live," ordered my aunt, "and
let them cook until they shrivel and turn steel blue."

Thus everything was made complete, and we went into the
incandescent dining-room to join our guests.

The English aesthete, protégé of my blonde cousin Adorian, and
Madeleine, adored but adopted daughter of the childless union of
the Count Adolphus and the Countess Ada, were the only visitors
I did not recognise from an earlier year.

"My dear, you look absolutely *ravissant*," said myopic Countess
Ada, "you simply must meet Madeleine."

However, before that happened the implacable gong gave out
with sonorous tidings of the approaching pabulum and, at the
sound, we all took our places, according to the established de-
corum, at the ebony table. I sat in velvet, as always, between my

aunt and the ageing mistress, so old as to have been long accepted as a second or rather parallel wife, of General X. The Garbure Béarnaise was served in ochre bowls of rough clay, the Truites au Bleu came on dishes of silver garlanded with circles of lemon and round potatoes, and the Grives au Genièvre were carried high on plates of the finest porcelain. The bones crunched delicously beneath white teeth, knives and forks flashed like smiles as they moved, faces shone, and the wine glowed like a living thing in the crystal glasses. Then amid a fanfare of the oohs and aahs of aroused and admiring appetites the Canard au Sang was brought on and, as Uncle Vlad flamed the pieces of meat with the sauce of blood and wine and a bottle of cognac, I looked toward Madeleine for the first time.

Her face was the shape of a slightly more serious moon than our own, and her nocturnal hair was as black as the ravens that fly in the hills beyond our lands. She seemed to be searching some distant horizon, for her crescent eyebrows hovered like the wings of a gliding bird, and her mouth was slightly open as if she were holding the most delicate bird's egg between her lips. When she noticed that I was regarding her so curiously she smiled a little and she blushed.

As was the custom, after the main course, our smooth glasses were filled with champagne, and we left the decadent table, before the dessert was served. The wonders of our cuisine were praised, by a familiar chorus, to the heights of our moulded ceilings; but my aunt went outside with the English aesthete to discuss synaesthesia, and Uncle Vlad took the opportunity to catch some moths. I looked for Madeleine, but I could not find her.

"I say, young fellow," mumbled ancient Count Adolphus through his moustaches, "have you seen Madeleine yet?"

But I did not see Madeleine again until the butterflies burst into ardent applause when we all sat down for the Crêpes aux Papillons. There was something indescribably wonderful, that night, in watching those blazing palettes puff away in smoke; it was very much as if the colours evaporated into the air and were absorbed by our breath. The crêpes too seemed suffused with this vibrant energy; it must be said, Uncle Vlad had created the most brilliant dessert of his life. I wondered afterwards if the extraordinary vitality had communicated itself to Madeleine, if her cheeks had grown roses, but when I looked I saw that she was already walking away from the table.

"I do believe that that young lady has dropped her handkerchief," observed the mistress of General X. "If I were you, young man, I should return it to her."

I nodded. I could hear the violins beginning to play discordant themes in the ballroom.

The dance opened with a grand flourish of wind instruments and took off around the room on the resonant wings of the flutes and strings, and joined, in counterpoint, the butterflies released simultaneously by Uncle Vlad. My uncle and aunt, as much concerned with the macula lutea as with the more alimentary organs, had carefully planned to fill in the musical space with the most unusual sights. A pellucid cube of the purest crystal was suspended from the centre of the ceiling and rotated on a fixed cycle by means of a concealed clockwork motor, creating an optical illusion, for in each of the faces a single eye was carved, and in each of the eyes a prism had been planted; so that, as it revolved above the dancing floor, it caught the occasional beam of light and projected visionary rainbows. Benevolent Uncle Vlad, having led the dancers with my aunt in an energetic pas de deux, stood resting against an ormulu commode, pouring out tall glasses of punch from a commodious bowl, happily recording the performance of his decorated insects.

"Ah, Nephew," he remarked as I emerged from among a crowd of dancers, "have you noticed that spinal quiver in the little beasts when a certain note is sounded, high C, I believe?"

"As a matter of fact I have not," I replied. "I am trying to find Madeleine to return a handkerchief."

Countess Ada and Count Adolphus came capering by and called out, "She is beside the flowers in the garden."

Madeleine was standing all alone beneath the moon, in the centre of a crazy path, skirted by a row of yellow gaslights and ghostly trees. As I approached nearer to her, along that long lane, I fancied that she was looking, as if fascinated, at the illuminated cupolas, each of which was nightly adorned with the tingling jewellery of bats. And I was reminded what a newcomer Madeleine really was, for this singular display was almost a family phenomenon; indeed, by coincidence, all true members of our family have a small but distinctive brown birth mark on the cheek that is said to resemble two open wings. Poor General X, as a result of this, was forced to grow a bushy beard, not because of his military manner, nor because of his virile dignity, but because he developed an unfortunate twitch.

"Hello," I spoke into the night, "hello." I do not think that I have seen anyone look so beautiful as Madeleine looked at that moment with the full curve of her throat outlined against the blackness as if by the inspired stroke of an artist's brush.

She jumped a little, like a sleeper awakened, and turned towards me. Her brown eyes were excited and shining like an indian summer. "The night is so wonderful," she said, "I feel enchanted."

"Let us walk together," I replied, "and I will show you the garden."

Madeleine took my arm and in the instant that I felt the warm flesh of her own bare arm brush carelessly against my cold hand I experienced a sensation I can only call an emotional tickle; as if some hitherto secret nerve end had been suddenly revealed and stimulated. That arm of hers was a marvellous thing, it was no single colour but a multitude of hues and tints, and covered with the finest down, except inside the elbow, where the smooth skin was pale and shy and utterly desirable. The flowers were everywhere but the famous roses were all spaced out before the french windows, so that they encircled the building like some blooming necklace. Madeleine reached out to pick one of the blossoms but managed only to prick her finger. She gave a little cry, and stared at the finger which was rapidly dropping beads of blood.

"Let me see," I said, "I know how to make it better." And I took the wounded finger between my thumb and forefinger and squeezed it, very carefully, until the last few drops of blood came like red flowers, then I carried it to my lips and sucked away any hurt. I bandaged the flushed tip with Madeleine's own handkerchief.

She smiled.

"Will you dance?" I asked.

The slight dizzyness I had felt when I tended Madeleine's hurt was heightened by our mazy movement around the dance floor to the sound of a jazzy waltz; though it was not, in fact, at all an unpleasant feeling, rather like being drunk on champagne bubbles.

"Look!" shouted Countess Ada to my aunt. "Look who Madeleine is dancing with."

Madeleine coloured slightly, which only made her the more radiant, then as she raised her face to me the spectrum burst all over her, and all else retreated into spectral shades. In the magic of that moment I completely forgot that the entire illusion was due to the clever artifice of my uncle and aunt and quite unconsciously pulled Madeleine closer to me, she responded with a shiver along her back, as if she were waving invisible wings, and I drifted over a dream-like sea holding on to Madeleine's warm body. I have no idea how long that moment lasted, but in those seconds or minutes I experienced an extraordinary sensation: my senses were literally magnified, I saw her skin as mixtures of pure colour, I felt her every movement; the beat of her heart, the air in her lungs, the blood in her veins. But Madeleine suddenly broke the spell.

"Oh, no!" she cried. "We have danced over a butterfly."

When, at last, a sliver of sun shone through the leadlight windows and exploded over the trumpet section, the dancers all leaned against one another and walked from the floor into the corridors and dimness of the receding night. I led Madeleine by the hand to her chamber.

"I must sleep now," she said, "but we will meet again in the afternoon?"

"Yes, you must sleep," I replied as I touched her tired eyelids with my fingertips, "but I will plan a picnic for when you awaken, and I will show you the ruined castle of Vled." I returned to the ballroom to find my uncle and aunt, to congratulate them upon their success, and found them both upon their knees collecting up the bruised bodies of the fallen butterflies. I joined them, to complete the family group, crawling about as if we were posing for a portrait of a surreal autumn in a sparkling land of leaves without trees.

"Your designs were wonderful, the execution was superb," I

said to them both, "even I ignored the methods for the sake of the effect."

"Everything worked perfectly," agreed my aunt, "and what is more you and Madeleine liked each other."

"Yes, I wanted to speak to you about that," I began. "I have asked Madeleine to come with me beyond the woods, and I would like to take some food and wine with us," I paused, "so will you be kind enough to show me the cellars?"

Uncle Vlad looked very pleased with himself and beamed at my aunt as if all credit for my request was owed to him. "Of course, with pleasure," he replied, with that smile of his, and added: "Tell me, Nephew, do you intend to kiss her?"

No light at all came into the cellars except, that is, from the illumined rectangle at the head of the stairs, where the old oaken door was left open. I had never been into the cellars before, so it was all strange to me, but Uncle Vlad walked among the rows upon rows of green bottles as if this weird underwater world were his natural habitat.

"We are standing directly beneath our small lake," he informed me. "The cellars were designed that way deliberately so as to control the air temperature in here."

Soon I was moving about freely on my own, and the longer I remained in the cellars the more I felt that I too belonged to this profound environment, that I was in truth the nephew of my uncle. The air was rich with the smells of the earth, the cellars were like a distillation of night and the world, the essence of the veil, the antithesis of those bright tedious rooms where everything is visible at once, where you forget that you are breathing. There should be an art to capturing beauty; it becomes merely banal when it is not hunted. Uncle Vlad emerged from the depths of a particularly dusty rack of vintage carrying two bottles of red wine by their swans' necks, one in each hand.

"These should be just the thing," he said as he rubbed a label, "Château Margaux."

Then we went much deeper, beyond where the wine was stored, until we came to a dank natural cave which smelt very strongly of pelardon. Uncle Vlad picked up a few small rounds of the aged goats' cheese, carefully wrapped and tied in dusky vine leaves, and weighed them in his hands. "Perfect," he adjudged, "just ripe. Now all you require is some pâté de foie gras."

"You must beware of the sun," said Madeleine, regarding my pale complexion with some concern, "I do not want you to burn because of showing me the castle."

She gave me her straw bonnet to wear, and the blue ribbons flew in the breeze on the slope of the hill. Lupus, the great dog, ran on through the waving corn and the poppies and waited for us, barking, at the start of the woods. Several birds flew out in a straight line squawking with alarm. The woods were much cooler and greener than the sandy daylight, a delightful diurnal anachronism, an eden free from gardeners; what is more, I knew all the paths. Lupus darted ahead and chased rabbits through the undergrowth; usually he caught them. I carried the picnic on my back in a creamy satchel made from a pelt of the softest goatskin, and led Madeleine by the hand, watching all the tonal variations that the light and the shade of the sun and the different leaves made over her body. It seemed that the life in her had come to the surface and was showing itself in this ebb and flow of moving colours. I chose the spot very carefully and spread a chequered cloth over the ground, and I put out all the food on it in the crafty design of a rather ingenious check mate. We sat beneath the tall trees in the long grass. The picnic was excellent; the pâté provided the expected largesse, the cheese had just the right temperament, and I continually filled the glasses with the flowing wine. Madeleine ate a yellow pear for her dessert, and the juice dripped from her fingers; her black hair was just touching emerald leaves, also pear-shaped, and the attracted flies flew round her head like a halo.

"That was a lovely picnic," she said, smiling. "What shall we do now?"

"I must tell you something, Madeleine," I confessed, by way of a reply, after some assumed consideration. "I dabble in paronomasia."

Madeleine put down the core of the pear. "I thought that the game would be chess," she gave me a sly smile, "but now I suppose that it will be a crossword puzzle, am I right?"

She was right, of course. Nevertheless, I took a black crayon

from the satchel and wrote on the white squares of the cloth —
many alive devils enliven living even in novel evils.

"Oh, well," laughed Madeleine, "we all have our acrostics to
bear."

I don't know why, it certainly was not because Madeleine had
beaten me at my own game, but her response made me shiver.
Madeleine must have noticed because she touched my cheek with
her lips.

"You are cold," she said.

"There," I said after we pushed through the last of the overgrown bushes, "is Vled's castle."

The ruined keep stood erect and solitary on the motte in melancholy grandeur. Ravens flew about the grey merlons in great
circles. As we watched, the setting sun shone red through holes in
the broken walls giving the whole, for a brief while, the appearance
of a cavernous skull with bloodshot sockets. Although I had seen
the same sight many times it still exerted over me an irresistible
and hypnotic fascination; as if there really were some powerful
force behind those empty carmine eyes. Then the sun deepened to
purple and streaks of fiery clouds opened labial wounds in the sky.
The castle looked even blacker, and all the more compelling. Madeleine did not blink, she stood transfixed, staring into the approaching gloom; her eyes reflected what she saw. I felt her hand tighten
in mine and grow colder all the time; her entire being seemed
frozen on the threshold of an irreversible event like a reluctant
swimmer poised on the edge of a diving board. I touched her left
breast with my right hand, just enough to feel the flesh.

"Will you go in, Madeleine?" I asked. She came without a
word.

The graves of my ancestors were all covered with historic weeds,
and the moat was dry, but a wooden table and twelve wooden
chairs remained within the hollow keep. We walked through the
grounds with all the care and respect due to fallen stones and
came into the dining hall. It was evening. I lit many candles and
covered the table with the chequered cloth and spread out upon
it the remains of the picnic; there were a few cheeses, a little pâté,
much fruit, and most of a bottle of wine, so that I was able to
compose a creditable still life. It glowed in the glimmering light.

On the walls beside where Madeleine sat there was the famed mural which represented, in picturesque detail, the narrative of Vled's many military victories, also, by way of interludes, either for himself or the spectator, the artist had included the faded delights of Vled's more carnal conquests. Even as I looked a single moonbeam suddenly shot as swift as an arrow through a crack in the annals and flashed directly on to Madeleine's face and neck.

"This is the most extraordinary supper," she murmured, very coyly, "that I have ever eaten." She smiled across at me and I saw at once, in the luminous night, that her upper lip was shaped exactly like the famous long-bow old Vled had used to lick the Turks. It quivered a little beneath my gaze, and the more I studied that priceless object the more I was filled with an increasing need to make it mine. I wanted to taste that secret egg. Then the light changed, or she moved. I followed the graceful arch of her neck to where her ear disappeared among her rich hair and I felt again, though I knew not why, that I had to possess that mysterious lobe that hung so full like a liquid jewel. Madeleine became in that chance instant of illumination a collection of individual treasures and temptations; I had never done it before, but I knew then that I had to kiss her. My desire was inevitable, as inevitable as the flame that burned above the candle.

In the courtyard beyond the keep, in the centre of a thirsty fountain, a small statue of Cupid was slowly falling to pieces.

There is an old belief in our family to the effect that any passion, if held strongly enough, can so influence the prevailing atmosphere as to establish conditions favourable for the realisation of that same passion. It happened in the gathering night that Madeleine got up from her place at a table of crumbling foods and walked towards me, slowly, languorously, through the undulant waves and splashes of candlelight and wax. I couldn't take my eyes from her mouth; the tongue was just visible through the open lips; the teeth looked sharp and white. I rose too, unawares, in a state of hard anticipation. We met, quickly, flesh against flesh; and I knew, by a kind of ecstatic instinct, exactly what I had to do.

I put my hands on Madeleine's hot cheeks, making a prize cup of my hands and her cervix, and tilted her head to one side. She looked at me with a sleepy look, and half closed her eyes. Her lips started to move. I placed my face on Madeleine's offered neck and began to kiss her, moving my tongue over her smooth skin, seeking, seeking, pressing, until I could feel the blood pumping through her jugular vein. Then I took a roll of the powdered flesh between my lips so that it was pressed against my teeth. I had to hold Madeleine tight, for her whole body was swept again and again with a series of short but violent tremors. I could feel her breathing right into my ear, her warm breath came in gasps and clung to me for a few seconds before vanishing. I sank my teeth into the skin and pushed, harder, harder — suddenly a great wave seized me and with a convulsive spasm of my cervical spine I bit deeper into Madeleine's vein. Then my mouth was filled with her blood and I think I heard her shriek of pleasure through my own blaze of delight.

It was a perfect kiss! I kissed Madeleine until I had to stop for breath; by then she was quite relaxed, and the arms which had clutched me so firmly hung limp by her sides. I carried her gently to the table and rolled her over the chequered cloth so that she finished on her back. Her arms got in a bit of a tangle, so I straightened them out for her. And I leaned back in a chair, well satisfied. As I did so a rather large *acherontia atropos* flew into a candle flame and fell burning on to Madeleine's cheek. She was too weak to brush it off; her hands fluttered as vainly as the moth's wings.

"Madeleine," I whispered in her ear as I blew off the ashes, "now you are really one of the family."

THE PROMISED LAND

Call me Schlemiel. You will after you've read this.

First let me tell you about my affair with Hannah Ratskin, I should have been so lucky.

Well, Hannah lived in Tel Aviv. We're in Israel, you understand. I'm some miles away, in Jerusalem, on holiday. So one day I go to visit Hannah. I have a quick *mitz tapuzim* — orange juice — at the bus station, look longingly at the *avatiah*, red wet slices of mouth-watering watermelon, then shove my way aboard a number 5, hanging on to a strap all the way along Allenby and Dizengoff, finally getting off at Arlosoroff. Hannah's apartment is around the corner, on Weizman.

She is pleased to see me. "You must stay the night," she says. "It'll have to be on the couch," she adds, "unfortunately my bed is already occupied."

Enter Ami Ben Tur: handsome, Israeli; curly-haired scion of a wealthy family. The noise he causes when he *shtups* Hannah keeps me up half the night.

The phone wakes me. Hannah answers it. Word has reached her parents that I have spent the night in her flat. For some reason they detest me; the idea that I may have fucked their daughter fills them with horror. They are on their way to see for themselves. Since they live around the corner I have very little time to decamp. I rush downstairs and hide behind a tree in the back garden. The neighbours come to see what I'm doing there. I cannot tell them because the Hebrew I've learned from Rivka, my teacher, has not equipped me for such an eventuality. I give the Ratskins plenty of time to complete their interrogation, but even so my re-entrance coincides with their exit.

Mrs Ratskin looks me in the eye. "Did you spend the night with my daughter?" she says.

Of course I cannot bring myself to say "Yes", but it is equally impossible to say "No" since I am standing there in my pyjamas.

Upstairs Hannah is looking sick. "You can come out now," she says to Ami Ben Tur, who emerges naked from a wardrobe. What with all the tension I drink half a bottle of whisky, tell Hannah that I love her, and subside into some kind of coma on the sofa. Once again I am roused by the telephone. It is the Ratskins. They want to know if I have gone yet. They inform Hannah that if I sleep one more night in her flat they will stop paying her rent. Further, it is hinted that if he is not obeyed Mr Ratskin will have a heart attack.

"Do you want the death of your father?" cries Mrs Ratskin.

Hannah is distraught, she turns to me for help. "Please phone my father while we are out for dinner," she pleads, "and apologise."

I drink some more whisky. And while Hannah dines in luxury with her lover, probably while she's tucking into the avocado, I dial the number. Mr Ratskin tells me that he has nothing against me personally, he simply objects to the fact that my presence is corrupting his daughter, and doing nothing for her reputation. He repeats his ultimatum, and reminds me that he never goes back on a decision. I behave like a gentleman, and prepare to bow out. But I begin to feel more and more like a *nebbish*, a nothing. I phone back. This time Mrs Ratskin wants me to herself. She says that because of me Mr Ratskin is on the brink of apoplexy. I increase the danger straight away by saying that I have decided to stay. Let Hannah choose. In all seriousness I say I'll pay her rent. This is the last straw.

"What do you want from my daughter?" Mrs Ratskin demands. "I've seen your letters. I know that you love her. But she won't marry you. Don't you know that she has a boyfriend already? Ami Ben Tur. What must he think when he says goodnight, knowing you are sleeping in the flat? Why are you trying to divide our family? You have upset Mr Ratskin and I am sure you will upset Hannah when she hears what you have said. Why don't you go away?"

I put down the receiver. I feel a *mensh*.

I tell Hannah what I have done. She does not believe me. More phone calls, but no mercy. Hannah goes to bed with Ami Ben Tur.

He gives me a last look of contempt. I have violent diarrhoea. I sit on the toilet and hear Hannah have her orgasm in the next room. Some time afterwards she reappears in a diaphanous gown and while I stare at her breasts she phones her parents and informs them that she is going to marry Ami Ben Tur. I am now considered an irrelevance, indeed Mr Ratskin repeats that he never had anything against me personally. In the following days things happen fast; a ring is purchased, a banqueting room is booked at the Hilton, invitations are printed. I am not asked. Still Hannah takes time to confide in me.

"Do you know why I decided to marry Ami?" she asks.

"No," I say.

"Because he is the only man who has ever given me a vaginal orgasm," she says.

Right after the wedding Ami Ben Tur gets called up.

Hannah phones me. "Hello, Lem," she says, "I'm bored. Ami's away in Sinai and I've got nothing to do."

I plan my advance carefully. I go into the Old City to obtain some hashish (oysters for the contemporary Cassanova); I buy two full fingers. I catch a *sherut* from the corner of Ben Yehuda that'll take me into the centre of Tel Aviv, and as we drive through the hills around Jerusalem, passing the rust-proof wrecks of armoured cars and lorries, relics of the '48 war, I am polishing up my strategy for the final seduction of Hannah. It is my intention to stimulate her senses to such a degree that she will be compelled, both by her own desires and the overwhelming demands of her female hormones, to capitulate to your foolish narrator.

I'll tell you the theory. If alcohol is administered under the right conditions it invariably begins the process by which the perception of the drinkers is so altered that they become the participants in a series of events in which the only possible combinations are between those characters present — in this instance just Hannah and myself. It's a warm night and there's no problem getting Hannah tipsy. Our context is as sharply defined as is the world by a window-frame. I use the hashish to draw the curtains. But follow me, I'll lead you to a spot where you can peep through the glass.

You will see that the two personages have been swimming (a

midnight dip); that red-headed Hannah is still wearing a yellow bikini designed by a lascivious geometrician. Her breasts are yash-maked beneath two tiny isosceles triangles, each topped with the pluckable outline of a nipple near the pinnacle, from which points two yellow ribbons run, a pair of twin hypotenuses, to yoke the whole design with a bow behind her neck. Her private parts are concealed beneath another triangle, this one with much greater angles at the base, so that the sides point generously to her genitals. Please understand how impressed I am with this garment, which must have been as finely calculated as the Great Pyramid itself. Your narrator is not quite so contented with his own attire, since he has been compelled to borrow a pair of horrible scarlet briefs from Ami Ben Tur's wardrobe, so I must ask you to forgive me should my excitement become too apparent. I begin to unwrap warm giggling Hannah by tweaking her vital bow between thumb and forefinger, at which point all mathematical pretentions collapse to reveal a fine bosom, looking rather pale compared to the tanned surrounding skin, with just a hint of colour in the depressed mamillae. What I find beneath the mid-section is even more arresting, dozens of curls pressed flat into the white delta of her belly, the calm red waves of a naturally warm sea. Hannah is now riding the crest, of her own volition she slides a fidgety finger-tip along her dampening sex and sniffs. She giggles and puts her finger under my nose. Hannah herself removes Ami's trunks from my midriff and drops them on to the floor where they settle like a deformed grin. Things are certainly going to plan, I think.

I put some jazz on the record player. We undulate across the room to the sofa, in a sort of embrace, my tongue taking advantage of an open-mouthed kiss to say how-do-you-do to her soft uvula as well as sweet-talking her dangling epiglottis. Hannah sinks on to the sofa and before descending I look down on the land promised me long ago by that smile of hers. I loom over her sentient softness and kiss her constellar aureole, teasing her nipple till it is firm, then my tongue slips on slippery lips down the slope of her breast, beyond her knotty navel, through her salty pubic hairs into her fuzzy hive. I pause on the brink. By now Hannah is whimpering and rocking her body from side to side; it would be wicked to stop, so I close my eyes (I've always been a fussy eater)

and whisper her name, and as my tongue curls up on the final *ah*
I push it between her labia, and lap her up to the rhythms of
Charlie Mingus. Even in my darkness I know that her thighs and
calves are golden as though honey were overflowing. It's no time
for speeches, you'll agree, but gradually I become aware that
Hannah is saying something.

"Are we going to fuck?" she says.

This stops me in my tracks. "Aren't we?" I say.

"In that case I must tell you that I have stopped taking the
pill," says Hannah, "because we are going to start a baby. And
I'd like to be sure that Ami is the father. Have you any rubbers
with you?"

Of course I haven't!

"Why don't you just finish what you were doing," says Hannah,
making herself comfortable and opening her legs a bit wider.

So here I am on my knees with my tongue up Hannah and my
bum in the air when all of a sudden there's a commotion at the
window. Ami Ben Tur, on a surprise weekend pass, bursts in. As
is only to be expected, he threatens to kill me. Hannah screams. I
retreat in disarray from the occupied territories, with a cocked
Walther PPK pointing at my non-negotiable areas.

Half a year later there's a war on.

I'm in England at the time, in shul, on my annual visit, atoning
for my sins, hoping God accepts the English translation of his
prayers, when someone comes running in shouting, "Those
bastards have invaded Israel!" What a *mishegoss*!

A couple of days after, when it's clear how bad the fighting is,
I go to give a pint of blood at the same shul, now converted into
a blood transfusion centre. Inside there are about thirty clean beds,
each one supporting a passive pale individual joined by what looks
like an external vein to a reddening bottle. Nurses dressed in
white walk through dusty sunbeams smiling at the bleeding people,
while doctors have the sterner task of separating the Os from the
ABs. I'm just about to be dismissed on account of my hayfever
when it's discovered that I'm AB Rhesus-negative, very rare. So
they put me on some freshly laundered sheets, puff up my arm,
and stick a needle into a surprised vein just inside my elbow. It

is at about this time, I later learn, that Ami Ben Tur is hit in the stomach by a piece of shrapnel. He is rushed by helicopter to the nearest hospital where it is discovered that his blood-group is also AB Rh-negative. He is given many transfusions. I do not know if he is given my blood, but when I next see him he is sneezing.

For several years I have been going to Israel a month at a time, you understand, and I have yet to bed an Israeli girl. Hannah was by no means my only near-miss, there was also Rivka, my Hebrew teacher. Say her name to yourself; just listen to the smooth flow of the *riv* as it glides into the soft mound of the final *ka*. Ah, I can see myself now, the bright boy of the class, reciting for Rivka the conjugations of the verb *ohev*, to love. *"Ani ohev,"* I say: "I love," as metaphysical a statement as I'm ever likely to make. Anyway, as soon as the war breaks out Rivka's off to Israel like a shot, and I don't see her again till the following spring.

It's a hard job to find her house at Ramat Aviv, I can tell you. *"Slicha, efor Rehov Gruniman?"* I say to the locals, but cannot understand the reply. I don't blame Rivka, she didn't write the textbook after all, but outside of supermarkets my vocabulary is useless. There's one version of the Bible in which Moses attempts to extricate himself from God's command by stammering that his tongue is not circumcised. Well, that's exactly how I feel in Israel: I am Jewish, but my tongue is not circumcised. *"Ani lo mdaber ivrit,"* I say. I do not speak Hebrew.

"Thanks God," says Rivka, "you have arrived. I thought maybe you had got lost."

She brings me a slice of *avatiah*, and sits very close beside me, so that her thigh is pressed against my leg. This proximity imports an unfortunate element of insincerity into our conversation; for while I am speaking of one thing my mind is diverted by a different matter entirely. Rivka has become enamoured by Gush Emunim, the Greater Israel movement.

"We must not give back an inch," she says, "not of anywhere, especially Jerusalem." She then goes on to explain the importance of the land in this way: "Make a triangle with points at Ba' Am (North), Gaza (West) and Eilat (South), so that Jerusalem is located at the centre of the long base. Then make a second triangle around Sinai. Join the two and you have the Mogen David, the Star of David, symbol of Israel."

The eternal triangle, of which I already had much experience. "What about the Palestinians?" I say. I do not hear her reply because I am imagining myself infiltrating her panties (which I can see as clearly as the rights of the case I am arguing) and consuming her burning bush. Just look at me, the politician, the moralist with my spadix blooming in my spathes!

Rivka invites me to accompany her to Caesaria for a spot of sea-bathing. Surely I am going to make it now, consumate my love for the country for which I had so recently shed blood. Caesaria is the only beach I know along Israel's west coast where swimmers are not pestered by waves. For this pacific enclave in the Mediterranean specific thanks must be given to the Romans who enclosed the bay within stone breakers. The road down from the Tel Aviv-Haifa highway is littered with broken columns, pushed aside in places by orange trees from the new kibbutz. There is an agglomeration of ruins: Roman, Crusader, Moslem; a reminder, I say to Rivka, of the temporary nature of military conquests.

"Greeks, Romans, bah!" she says. "There were Jews in the time of the ancient Greeks, of the Romans, of the Phonecians. We are still here. Where are they? Our God is still God. Where is Zeus? I'll tell you, sneaking in the backdoor at Suez, like the Egyptians."

I shut up, and anticipate her bathing costume instead. She comes out of the changing room in a marvel of textile engineering; a backless strapless thing, looking like the letter q side-on; revealing a pleasing curvature on the reverse, extending from the nape of the neck over the vertebral rapids of the downy coccyx which merges into the tautologous material. We don't get back to Tel Aviv that night, but don't raise your hopes; Rivka wasn't that sort of girl.

She insists upon separate rooms in the small hotel we find. But during the night I hear a knock on my door and Rivka's there wrapped in a sheet. I follow her to her room, and she drops prone on to her bed. She is stark naked.

"Please do something," she says, "my back is on fire."

Sure enough her back is the colour of a spectacular sunset. Her bum, quivering a little, is as pale as a nocturnal creature; but I see her buttocks and her legs as the meeting of two question marks. Obeying instructions I dip my fingers into a tin of Nivea Cream and begin to massage the stuff into her back, moving in a circular fashion from the soft heights covering her clavicula, over the triangular deltoideus (a divine D, very relaxed), down through her central valley, then along her sides just touching on the periphery of her breasts, and down again over her ribs to the pelvic plateau, where I pause before going over her smooth hillocks (much cooler than the rest of her), feeling my breath come quickest where the going is easiest. The tempo diminishes during the descent of her legs, but speeds up again when I return to her thighs and make her gasp at last as my finger gets on to the sensitive flesh that remains (on this occasion) no man's land.

"Thanks God," says Rivka, "I feel better already." Such is the role of the diaspora in Israeli life.

I hope I haven't given the wrong impression about myself. I'm not really sex-mad, not very frivolous; in fact I'm rather a serious person. I've got this theory I want to tell you about; how it's materialism that's screwing us up. I mean real materialism, the belief that nothing exists but matter itself. Our trouble goes right back to the time when the Israelites, following Moses, got lost in the Sinai Desert. They were on their way to the Promised Land, you'll recall, the land "flowing with milk and honey", when they panicked and translated God's words into a Golden Calf — milk into a calf, honey into gold — needing to see before they could believe. I'm the same. I want to believe in miracles, in love-on-earth and life-after-death, but I turn all abstractions into flesh and stone. To tell you the truth, I want to fuck Israel. Okay, so Ahab was obsessed with Moby Dick; well, my Promised Land is only an Israeli cunt! Jesus, when I had my Bar Mitzvah they gave me a tree in Israel, I've got a certificate to prove it. Now I'm a big boy, a *mensh* even, so why won't they let me leave my own seed in a fertile belly?

Yes, I am serious. Look at me, I am interviewing A., the famous Israeli writer, for a magazine published by the Hebrew University. At first A. was reluctant to be interviewed without payment, until I told him that I was not being paid either. We are sitting opposite one another, in his living-room, sipping tea. No milk, no sugar.

Beyond us in the honeydew light the walls of Jerusalem glow.
When Jews pray they always face Jerusalem. I bend over my cup
and the steam infused with lemon rises like incense. A. has his
back to the city. A. is small but not delicate, compact; you'd guess
that he was either a poet or a boxer. In his fifties, I'd say. From a
generation that has survived wars and worse. Somehow wedded to
the land, those that died have become the land of course. He has
the dignity of a man whose suffering has not been self-inflicted.
Many writers espouse suffering, wear tragedy like a parrot on their
shoulder. A.'s poems come straight from the front-line. This is
my opinion, not a critical judgement. I switch on the tape-
recorder. Questions and answers are recorded. He prefers poetry
to prose. He has also led a life of action. In 1948 he ran guns for
the Hagganah. Sure, he has risked his life. Now he is secure and
famous. He recites a poem for me.

> " 'Never again will I find rest for my soul'
> Let me sit in the revolving chair
> of an AA gunner, of a pianist,
> of a barber, and I shall turn round and round
> restfully until my end."

The spool of my tape-recorder freewheels, the end of my tape
claps. The interview concludes, the baby-sitter arrives.

"Writing a novel," says A., "is like starting a marriage — in
the beginning you have no idea what you are letting yourself in
for." A. has recently begun a second marriage, the baby-sitter has
come to mind the evidence of his continuing creative powers.

"Shalom," we all say.

A.'s place is in *Yemin Moshe* — the Right Hand of Moses — a
higgledy-piggledy grouping of buildings, steps and alleys, the remains of the first modern Jewish settlement outside of the Old
City, now being lovingly restored. On a hillside, facing Mount Zion.
Beyond it is waste ground leading down to the valley of Gai
Hinnom (formerly Gehenna) where children were once sacrificed
to Moloch. I plan to walk across to the Jaffa Gate to catch an Arab
bus to Talpiot, but instead I just hang about in the shadows outside A.'s house. Above me a crescent moon continues to give a
weak grin.

A. returns. The baby-sitter leaves. I follow her through the alleys, over the waste ground, down toward Gai Hinnom. At the last moment she looks around and sees me, but before she can scream I am on her. She struggles. The tape-recorder drops with a thud and turns itself on. I hear A.'s voice: "Never again will I find rest of my soul." I prevail. No messing around with arithmetical underwear this time, or caressing claviculas. I rip her pants right off. No mistake, I rape her.

"Nazi!" she cries as I come.

"No," I say, shocked, "I'm a schlemiel."

A MOMENT OF
HAPPINESS

I live in fear. That's a state of mind, not my address.

Years ago I sat my exams at the Charles University. I had learned my work well and I was not nervous, until I saw the booklet that I was required to fill with my answers. I knew that in three hours it would be full, but I also foresaw the impossibility of my ever doing it; I felt that I was an insufficient motor to fulfil the inevitable. I tried to start the first question, but my hand was unable to control the pen. I could not form a single letter. Sweat began to roll along the lines on my hand and flow on to the page. I ran out of the hall. My sweat looked like teardrops on the page. All my professors were sympathetic, but they still failed me. Now no one will believe that I am an educated man.

It is six in the morning. Through my window I can see that the Vltava is turning gold with the rising of the sun. A beautiful sight, but I am immune to it; it fails to excite a single response in me. All it means is that it is time to move my bowels and to dress. Some days I am constipated, other days I have diarrhoea, less often I am regular. Every morning I examine the lavatory bowl, like an ancient sage, to see if I can divine what sort of day I have in store. This is fundamentally much more important than either the weather or the view. Today my movements have been very loose, which means I must pass the hours between now and bedtime in constant anticipation of further activity, presaging who knows what stomach complaint.

Once I discussed this morbid hypochondria with a doctor acquaintance and he, priding himself on his psychological insight, said that I did not trust my own body, would not believe that all those millions of interdependent functions could go on performing in harmony day after day without supervision. He accused me of introspective paranoia. Perhaps he is right. To me to get through a day is an achievement. As for the future, I have no faith in that at all. At best it is a process of gradual decomposition. I think only in the terms of the present and the past. I try to make the future as similar to the present as I can by sticking rigidly to an established dogma: I always get out of bed on the same side, I eat the same breakfast, I buy the same food in the same shops. My only desire in this life is to be a character in a photograph: smiling with remembered pleasure, eternally fixed in the present.

In many ways today is not normal. I have to work. *Rude Pravo* has a bold red headline: "PLNY ZDAR XV SJEZDU STRANY!" It is, of course, the start of the XVth Party Congress. And my beloved Prague is full of flags; equal numbers of Czech flags and Russian flags. To mark the occasion our local shop is unusually well-stocked with imported fruit; grapefruit, oranges, bananas and pineapples. This glut, which lured me into over-indulgence, must explain this morning's diarrhoea (I have been a second time). My job, which is going to last the whole of this week, requires me to stand beside a stall piled high with miniature Czech and Russian flags. This is situated outside (of all places!) the Pan American office. I sell a few flags, but mostly people ignore me and look at the posters in the window which say, "Come to the USA and help us celebrate our Bicentennial". On the opposite side of the street a peasant woman in head-scarf and embroidered apron is hawking painted eggs for Easter. When someone buys one she nicks the top and bottom off the shell and pulls a ribbon through it. I do not have much appetite, but I eat a little lunch: garlic sausage, a pickled cucumber and some rye bread. Afterwards I have to go to the toilet again.

In the afternoon the sun goes behind a black cloud and I begin to feel chilly standing around in the street. I notice a couple walking towards me carrying the English edition of Ctibor Rybar's guide to Prague. I approach them waving a Russian flag and ask, "Do you wish to exchange money?" I can see that this has surprised them. They have been saying "no" to money-changers all day, but I have got them off guard.

"I will give you forty crowns to the pound," I say. This is twice the official rate.

There is a moment's hesitation, then they ask to change £10.

We complete the transaction in the Café Europa. I hate it there. It is supposed to look like a Parisian café but looks are nothing; nowadays it is full of riff-raff: gypsies and workmen from the new Metro. The waiters wear ill-fitting tuxedos and are rude to everyone. I do not understand how the authorities tolerate them; probably because they never enter the Café Europa. Very sensible. I was once served pork there that was off, and I ended up in bed for a week with terrible cramps. I assure the couple that it is an excellent place to dine. They order a glass of mineral water and a bottle of Coca-Cola. The girl tells me that a friend of theirs came to Prague, met a Jewess in the Staronova Synagogue, stayed with her nine days, and married her six months later. She shows me a clipping from the *New York Times*. It is an article the fellow has written about his trip to romantic Prague.

"For years Czech émigrés in New York and London had regaled me with memories of the beauty of Prague," I read. "The city itself claims the affection of the 1968 generation of emigrants who, often in the same breath, described the charms of its women and the bankruptcy of its politics." The piece makes me want to vomit. I do not recognise the city he is writing about. It may as well be Xanadu.

"Robert couldn't get to the shul quickly enough," says the girl. "I think he was hoping to meet an exotic Jewish girl for himself."

I look at this Robert more carefully and wonder how I did not see before that he is Jewish. I can tell by the sharp way his eyes are examining me. I do not like the Jews. They trust nobody but themselves. I can see that he is growing suspicious of me; he has noticed that my fingers are short and stubby. I have been told this is a sign that I am not a pleasant person. I sit on my hands. I smile at the girl and begin to explain that I was not always this insignificant.

"I once worked for Cedok," I say, "and I used to take tours all over Eastern Europe. But in 1969 they gave me an important tour to Italy. And this, I must tell you, was my downfall. You know why? It is very simple. I went out with twenty persons and I came back with four. On the last day, at Trieste, I am sitting in the coach waiting for my party and only these four turn up. The rest want political asylum! And you know what? The coach driver also vanished. They had to send me out a new driver. When we returned at last I was fired. Just like that. Is it my fault people want to leave this country? I tell you, it's got so bad now that no one trusts anyone anymore. Everything must be a big secret!"

The girl is sympathetic, but that Robert is weighing up in his mind whether he should believe me. Well, it is the truth! I happen to know that a Cedok guide was sacked for losing practically a whole group in the West.

The staring eyes of the Jew have made me afraid. I make an excuse and hastily leave the café. There's no real reason, I've told those stories many times before. But walking back to my rooms, without warning, my stomach turns to water. I feel dizzy. I know every stone in the street but I lose all confidence in my ability to get to the other end. I begin to run, to race my fears, imagining fearful phantoms lurking in the shadows, the secret policemen of my subconscious, trying to grab me. To arrest me for what? For being a fraud, a counterfeit man? A drunk full of Pilsner staggers towards me. He nods to me as if in recognition of a fellow sufferer. Madness! I do not suffer. But even as I turn the corner I know that the drunk has straightened up and is watching me.

Next day I meet the couple again. I would rather not talk to them, but they seem anxious to tell me how much they have seen of Prague.

"This morning we saw the tomb of Rabbi Low," says the girl, "and we left a note with our names on it."

"Have you heard all about Rabbi Low and his famous Golem?" I ask. Surely they are not interested in that superstitious rubbish! Then I recall that Robert is a Jew. I consider telling him why the Nazis did not destroy the Prague ghetto. Because they wanted to preserve it as a museum of a vanished race. Now there are hardly any Jews left in Prague and the synagogues are maintained by the goverment as museums. And the chief sightseers are our wonderful East German comrades. Such ironies give me much pleasure.

The girl is still talking.

Ah, now what has Mr Robert got to say?

"One thing I miss, not being able to speak the language," he says, "is the fun of eavesdropping. When we get back we will be asked, 'What were the people like? Happy?' And all I will be able to say is that they looked like people: some looked pleased, others looked miserable. How am I supposed to tell what they are thinking?"

I am thinking: what if I were to accuse this Jewboy of being a Zionist and then rape his girlfriend? I nod sympathetically.

The girl pulls something out of her handbag and says, "Look what we bought with the money we changed yesterday."

It is an ancient coin, tiny and silver. What would anyone want with that?

"It's supposed to be a dinar of Vratislav II," says Robert.

Supposed! The suspicious kike. If he got it at Starozitnost's it *is* a dinar of Vratislav II.

"I'll tell you two something," I say confidentially, "on my mother's side my ancestors go right back to this Vrastislas II. He was the first real king of the Czechs, you know. Founded that monastery right up there on top of the castle. Strahov. Yes, I was once a person of high rank. I had money. When I was seventeen I inherited our family estates. They were worth something in the order of half a million. In those days, you can imagine! Well, I made a fantastic success of it. Implemented so many reforms in forestry that I was awarded an honourary degree in agriculture from Charles University. Then came the war. And you can guess what happened after. The communists have it all now."

A person approaches me to buy a Russian flag. I think it's a fellow. I look more carefully and see he's got a huge chest, like a hunchback turned round. Daft! They're tits. I look at the person's face again and see that it is a very ugly girl. I think: what sort of life can she lead?'

Robert wants to know about some book. He says he has been asked to get it for a friend. He reads me the title from a notebook. *Vabank* by Alexej Pludek. Why should anyone he knows outside of Czechoslovakia want such trash? Perhaps he mixes with dissidents. In his notebook I glimpse the address of someone in Prague. Perhaps if he is taking out something he also brought in something. Something like illegal manuscripts. I memorise the address; tonight I will telephone it to the police.

"Ah, you want to buy *Vabank*," I say. "You know it has just been awarded our National Book Prize? It's all about Zionism. About the plot, begun in 1967 with the Six-Day War, continued in Czechoslovakia in 1968, and so on, for Jews to seize the governments of all the major world powers. A novel way of looking at the events of 1968, don't you agree? Oh! I believe I have just made a pun."

I am beginning to enjoy myself. But both of my friends are looking uncomfortable. They do not know if I am serious or not.

"I am not against the State of Israel, you understand," I say, "far from it. But I think it should only be a homeland for Hebrews. Not Khazars. You see, most people who call themselves Jews are really Khazars, descendants of a Black Sea tribe who converted to Judaism for political reasons and then dispersed through Europe. These are the people of the diaspora, not the Hebrews."

What can they reply to that?

"I'll tell you something else," I say, "about the Dead Sea. We're all led to believe that it's dead because it's full of salt. Yes! But no one says that there are ten different mineral salts in it. I'll tell you something. Those salts are worth more than America's entire annual gross national product. How do I know? Well, I spent years working on the Dead Sea. But I was forced to supress my findings. Because what I knew would have started a Holy War! *Jihad*, the Arabs call it. On the strength of rumours of my work I was offered the directorship of Amman University. It is all documented. I have the letters at home somewhere."

It is apparent that Robert does not believe a word I am saying. He is not attempting to argue or contradict, he just wants to get away from me as quickly as possible. But I am enjoying myself too much. Did I not sense it was going to be a good day when I laid that near-perfect shit this morning?

"My brother, you know, is looked on by the Arabs as a Prince," I inform the pair, "a fake one, of course, like Lawrence of Arabia. He entered Cairo as a sergeant in the Aussie army sometime in forty-four — oh, yes, he got out of Czechoslovakia in late thirty-eight — and right away met this little Arab boy. Hamil. And Hamil asks, 'What's your name, sergeant? You look more like one of us than an Aussie.' And my brother says, 'Saladin.' You see, it's the first Arab name that comes into his head. Hamil looks at him, and runs off. About an hour later there's two thousand Arabs knocking on his quarters crying, 'Saladin!' And Hamil says to my brother, 'I've brought all your relatives to see you.' I have to tell you that on a certain day of each year all the members of the Saladin family meet in Cairo. The very day that my brother showed up. There had been rumours. Stories that the head of the family had escaped the great massacre and fled to Australia. And here he was, returned. The next day there were newspaper headlines this high saying: 'Prince Saladin is Back!' After that my brother stayed on in Cairo. He became an agent. He got behind German lines. Smuggled hashish and secrets. When the war was over he became the leader of twenty thousand students. I'll tell you, if it wasn't for my brother the whole of Cairo would have burned down in fifty-two. You've heard of the Fires of Cairo? But my brother held his men under control. Nevertheless, Nasser had him tortured and thrown out. He was afraid of him."

All dictators fear men who are popular. They must watch over the State like I monitor my body. They must counter any abnormality with severe repression; anti-communists must be met with antibodies. Secret policemen are the penicillin of the nation. Like mould growing on the corpse of a loaf, there's a thought. When the body is purged the machine will run efficiently. I have heard that if ants cannot function properly they are taken away from the nest by three fellow workers and destroyed: one holds down its legs, another flattens its abdomen, and the third injects it with poison. I am no insect, but I am frightened. Not of Germans or renegades, but of invisible germs; of a revolution within. The State does its best to ensure control of the future, but there is no guarantee. The best it can do is rearrange the past to suit itself, and to stabilise the present in such a way that it becomes, simultaneously, a reflection of both past and future, thus liable to strict checks.

Six long black Russian limousines are edging down the road; the first flies the Hammer & Sickle. They are full of delegates to the Party Congress. Chubby men in grey homburgs with beige scarves in V's around their necks and black overcoats buttoned right up; chaperoned and chauffeured by secret-service men; immunised against the world. They give me reassurance, but what a joy it would be to assassinate one of them. Suddenly I understood how the germs that I destroy daily must feel.

The two English tourists are too intrigued by this procession of the powerful to bother much over my latest monologue.

"We must go now," says the girl in response to a look from Robert.

"Wait!" I say, "I have one last thing to tell you."

That's got them! No confessions from me, though. I have something else in mind.

"My brother lives in London now," I say. "I hear from him very often. He tells me that there is an excellent Czech restaurant in London. You must visit it. They serve magnificent knedliky. And schnitzels like you've never tasted. Not made with veal, but with pork that's been beaten flat till it's as thin as a pancake. Oooh, my mouth is watering. It is situated in Hampstead, West Hampstead. The Czech National House. You know of it? Our airmen who flew with the RAF founded it after the war was over. There is a photograph of the Queen on the wall encrusted with diamonds. How do I know this? My brother tells me. He also writes that all the Jews in Golders Green come and eat there every night, because they are smart, and they know when they are on to a good thing. You will go there? Undoubtedly you will see my brother. He looks just like me. Can you do me one favour? I see that you have a camera around your neck. Will you take a photograph of me for my brother?"

Robert opens his camera case. He fiddles with the exposure meter, sets the speed and the correct aperture. He places the camera to his eye and twists the lens until he has me in sharp focus. I smile. The shutter clicks. And so on a small piece of celluloid is a picture of me. Preserving me for that single 1/60th of a second in my life when I am not afraid.

WINGATE FOOTBALL CLUB

There are some dilemmas it is better not even to think about. I'll give you a for-instance. Suppose England were to play Israel in the World Cup. Who should I support? Ah, you will say, such a thing is very unlikely. England's football is stale, Israel's half-baked. But I'll tell you, stranger things have happened, like when Wingate won the London League Cup.

When I was a boy I used to go with my father to watch Wingate play on Saturday afternoons. Wingate were the only Jewish team in the entire football league; named in honour of our version of Lawrence, crazy Orde, a *goyisher* Zionist. Wingate were never a great team, and though they always had a couple of good players they usually spent the season near the bottom. So imagine our astonishment when we won a hard tie away from home and found ourselves in the London League Cup Final.

Our opponents were a dockland team, notorious for their anti-semitic supporters. They came to our ground like a wolf on the fold. But that year we had a brilliant outside-right, in real life a ladies' hairdresser. To me his dizzy runs down the wing were a thing of infinite beauty; left-backs tumbled to the ground when he passed, felled as if by magic. Pursued by these humbled clods he sprinted for the corner flag and unleashed acute crosses that sent their goalkeeper flailing in the air. Our centre-forward leapt and dived fearlessly to meet the winger's passes, but each time he missed by a hair's breadth.

"Only connect!" we yelled in encouragement.

The supporters of our opponents were prepared to tolerate our precocious start; content in the knowledge that Jews lacked spunk they waited for the crunching tackles to crush the life out of our challenge. And then our centre-forward did connect; his head met the pass fifteen yards out. The ball had "goal" written all over it as it shot like a bullet toward the net. The goalkeeper was frozen, as helpless as a rabbit, but — would you believe it? — even as we were celebrating the ball hit the post and rebounded back into the centre of the field. We cheered, nevertheless. But my father said sadly, "A miss is as good as a mile." And in my disappointment I felt the full force of the simile; all that marvellous approach-work had been for nothing because finally the ball had missed, the nearness of the miss didn't enter into it, a miss is as good as a mile.

A minute later I learnt another lesson. The rebound initiated an enemy attack which petered out harmlessly in the midfield mud, but then our centre-half made a disastrous error; although unchallenged he passed back to the goalkeeper, and to our horror the ball again stuck in the mud. It was a race for the ball between our goalie and their centre-forward, an ox. The goalie was first to the ball but before he could fully grasp it the centre-forward had crashed into him, not illegally, but carried by the momentum of his run. The ball spun from our goalkeeper's hands and bounced into the back of the net. We protested, hurled abuse at the referee, but the goal stood.

"Take note of that, young man," said the Prince of Shmattes who sported a velvet-collared camel hair overcoat. "It is an important lesson to learn: that the end justifies the means. We Jews have always been too fussy. When did pussyfooting around ever get us anywhere? Why can't our forwards barge into goalkeepers like that? Look at me. Did I make a success by tapping on doors? Not on your life. No, I barged straight in. Believe me, that's the only way to get on in this life."

Now that we were losing, the other side's supporters even cheered our outside-right and mocked their own left-back for being made to look foolish by the quicksilver jewboy.

The second half started with a sensation. Straight from the kick-off the ball went to our outside-right who rounded his man with arrogant ease and set off on one of his runs. At the last possible moment he crossed the ball and our centre-forward rose like there were springs in his heels to meet that perfect pass. He seemed to be floating while the ball rested on his instep before he smashed it into the back of the net. The equaliser! We went delirious with joy, we felt the exultation that perfection excites;

make no mistake, that goal was a work of art!

We breathed the ultimate in praise, "The goalie never stood a chance."

But try as they might Wingate just could not get that second all-important goal. Then ten minutes from time our right-half, laughingly overweight but astute with it, split their defence with a through ball which left our centre-forward alone with only the goalkeeper to beat.

"Shoot!" we pleaded.

He ran on, seemed to stumble, but kept his footing.

"Shoot!" we screamed.

But he hesitated. What was in his mind? Was he planning to dribble round the goalkeeper? However, before he had a chance to do a thing the goalkeeper suddenly rushed from his line and knocked him flat. The referee pointed to the spot. A penalty! Grown men, including my father, hid their faces as the centre-forward prepared to take the kick. This time there was no hesitation, before the tension had time to sink in the ball was in the goal. We could hardly believe it; less than ten minutes to go and we were ahead; we began to scent victory.

"WIN-GATE! WIN-GATE!" we chanted.

"How much longer?" I kept asking my father as the final minutes ticked away and the tension became unbearable. The attacks of our opponents grew increasingly desperate; their centre-forward charged again and again into our defence like a battering-ram. But our defence held. What a relief when the referee looked at his watch and put the whistle to his lips!

As the whistle blew a woman in a fake leopard-skin coat said out loud, "Hitler was right! Send the Jews to the showers!"

The boy standing next to her was one of our supporters (he looked big to me, but I don't suppose he was older than fourteen). "Keep quiet, you bitch!" he said.

Whereupon she slapped him round the face. He hit her back.

"You dirty Jew!" she cried.

Her companion moved in on the boy, but he never hit him more than once before Al Pinsky interceded. Now Al wasn't tall, so that golem just laughed, which was daft, because Al Pinsky was once the lightweight champion of Great Britain. The golem dropped the boy and took a swing at Pinsky. His fists were the size of hams. Pinsky ducked, like he was taking a bow, then straightened up and calmly knocked the fellow cold. When the police came and listened to the various versions of the incident we tingled with the pleasure of righteous indignation. That evening as I walked home with my father toward the awaiting glass of milk and toasted chola I felt elated; we had not only won the cup but also a great moral victory over the *yoks*. They had called us dirty Jews and we had stood up to them and got away scot free; on the contrary, it was they who left with bloody noses.

Now I realise that part of the fun of going to Wingate was the possibility of encountering just such anti-semitism. Among our supporters it was axiomatic that if you scratch a *goy* you'll find an anti-semite; our world-weary version of Shylock's great lament. Perhaps we had the mentality of people who go to the zoo to tease a caged lion and complain when it tries to bite them; but I think we welcomed the anti-semitism because it proved that we were morally superior; it may have confirmed our status as outcasts but it also reaffirmed our role as the chosen people. Although our daily existence gave us no evidence to support the fact there obviously was *something* different about us. And on Saturday afternoons we could flaunt this difference with pride, knowing that it would be recognised; we were the Wingate Supporters Club; our badge was the Mogen David. On the field our boys gave as good as they got, and on the sidelines if the *yoks* wanted trouble they could have it from us wholesale.

A couple of weeks after we won the cup, as if to rub in our moral superiority, the *Daily Mirror* ran an exposé on the horse-doping racket, and it turned out that most of the opposing team and many of their supporters were involved, including their centre-forward and the *shiksa* in the leopard-skin coat. That Saturday we were full of the news; it was too good to be true, not only were they anti-semites they were criminals as well!

"What else can you expect from *yoks* like that?' said the Prince of Shmattes.

My father, a wittier man, said, "*Goys* will be *goys*."

Of course my ambition was to play for Wingate. Every evening after school I would go into our backgarden and chase a football around. I divided myself into two imaginary teams; the first mounted dazzling attacks down the flank which were finished off by a deadly striker, and if a goal was not perfect they would not count it; the other was made up of plodders, grateful for any rebound or accidental goal they were without grace and had no time for the brilliant individual. The first team did not necessarily win, but they were always a pleasure to watch. As I ran I daydreamed of being the prince of outside-rights; the outsider who hovers on the periphery of the match but whose brilliant interventions win the day. What better ambition for a Jewish boy?

Our games master at school had flaming red hair and a beak of a nose, though he wasn't Jewish. Since my natural expression was one of discomfort I was his constant butt.

"Stop looking like you are suffering," he would say. "Boys are supposed to enjoy games."

My passion for football came as a surprise to him; in fact I was fleet-footed enough to be a good outside-right.

"Not bad," he said, "I didn't think your people liked physical activity." He took a look at my expensive football boots and said, "I bet your father earns a lot of money, eh?"

"I don't know," I said. I hadn't been going to watch Wingate for nothing; I knew an anti-semite when I saw one. Because I enjoyed football I was spared actual physical torment. However, my friend Solomon was a different kettle of fish. Solomon hated all games, especially football.

Poor Solomon was a coward, and Beaky sensed this at once. He picked out the six biggest louts in our class and told them to stand in a line. Then he threw the ball to Solomon and ordered him to run at them. Solomon didn't move. He was too scared even to argue.

"Get going you milksop, or else," said Beaky. Still no action from Solomon. So Beaky hit him, hard round the head. "You have no choice, you greasy tub of chopped liver," said Beaky.

Milchik or *flayshig,* it made no difference to him. Solomon ran at the boys in the line, kicking the ball far ahead of him, but not one of the boys bothered to go for the ball, taking their cue from their master they took Solomon instead. While Beaky watched they beat him up; not badly, but enough to make him cry. I make no excuses for my inactivity, I was only glad it wasn't happening to me; besides it was a part of our games lesson.

About the time I went away to university things began to go wrong for Wingate; lacking enough Jewish boys to make a *minyan* they had to co-opt non-Jewish players. It was true that Wingate was supposed to foster good-fellowship between Jewish and non-Jewish footballers, but most of our supporters felt this was going too far; this was — bite your tongue — assimilation. Gradually they stopped coming to watch Wingate and sure enough, as they had prophesied, the club lost its identity. The last time I saw them play the team was made up of strangers, men with names like Smith and Williams. The old atmosphere was gone. Wingate had become just another football team. At university I would continue to listen to the football results on the radio, but I could never feel for any other team what I had felt for Wingate; that sense of personal involvement was gone for ever. But by then I knew that there was more to life than football.

My parents assumed I had gone to university to get a degree, but I really went to lose my virginity. I became educated as a by-product. I discovered that the seminars were the great showplaces. So I made myself shine. Society functions were another good place to meet girls. I picked up Linda at the Jewish & Israel Society. Linda called herself the most experienced virgin in the western hemisphere; she would allow any physical intimacy short of intercourse. We slept together frequently, and sometimes I would get such a belly-ache from frustration that I could hardly stand up straight. In public we acted like lovers, but we were just going through the motions, like footballers without a ball. Still, thanks to Linda, I learned all about the role of the kibbutz in Israeli life. Not to mention the role of the Arab, the artist, the woman, the socialist and the *frum* Jew. One night a real Israeli came to speak. I had never seen a sabra before. He was swarthier than I expected. His subject was the role of peace in Israeli life. He was optimistic. He pointed out that it was now over a decade since Suez, and while there was no de jure peace there was clearly a de facto modus vivendi. A policy of live and let live. He believed that the Arabs had come to accept the presence of Israel, and that given time a normal relationship would develop between the former enemies. Had he got the wrong number!

When the Six-Day War began we didn't know that it was only going to last six days, of course. What trauma there was in the diaspora! No one gave Israel a chance. Every night we saw a different Arab army on the news. Their leaders promised to drive the Jews into the sea. Then Abba Eban would appear, sounding like a Cambridge don. The words of the Prince of Shmattes came back to me. "We Jews have always been too fussy. When did pussyfooting around ever get us anywhere?" Even Solomon's mother knew better than Abba Eban what was what.

"The Israelis should give the Arabs a bomb already," she said, "they should only suffer one hundredth of what we Jews have been through." She looked about ready to *plotz*.

No wonder, her son was in the Israeli army. After school, instead of going to university, Solomon had emigrated. We still kept in touch. He had a room in Jerusalem. Till the war-fever got me this had been my only real contact with Israel. But now it was time to separate the Jews from the *goys*. Of course I couldn't enlist in the Israeli army but I volunteered to go out as a driver of tractors or — God forbid — ambulances. I was warned that I might come under fire, but I brushed aside the possibility. However, my services were never required. The war ended too quickly.

It made for excellent television. Don't forget, it was my first war; I was too young to remember Suez. Every night I went to the television room next to the library to watch the late news. It was marvellous, our side were winning victory after victory. Films showed tanks scooting over the Sinai desert; the enemy were nowhere in sight. Soldiers hugged and kissed beneath the Western Wall of liberated Jerusalem, looking like they had just scored the winning goal. Experts explained with the aid of mobile diagrams the brilliance of the Israeli strategy; the daring raids, the lightning strikes. I had not felt such exultation since Wingate took the London League Cup; but I was older and I savoured my triumph in silence. Linda, beside me, was less circumspect. She screamed, she cried. I told her to shush, because we were not alone. Sitting by himself, the only other person in the room, was an Arab. Night by night his expression became progressively gloomier. When, on the seventh day, news came in of the Syrian atrocities, the captured Israeli pilot decapitated in front of the cameras and worse, he got up and walked out. "What do you expect from Arabs?" said Linda.

Solomon's mother telephoned, *shepping naches*; her song was my son the hero. His next letter was modest enough, but it made me envious. Of all people, Solomon had become glamorous! An outside-right, as it were. Such madness, to feel deprived because I had missed a war! But both Linda and I were engulfed in the exuberant aftermath. We discussed the possibility of marriage. We planned to become Israeli citizens. My Jewish destiny was about to be fulfilled.

Or so I thought. But chance took control; I was offered a post at the university, too good an opportunity to be missed. My destiny was postponed. Many other things also happened; governments fell, El Fatah became fashionable, Germany were revenged upon England in the Mexico World Cup, my parents celebrated their silver wedding, Linda and I were married. We went to Israel for our honeymoon. Naturally we visited Solomon in Jerusalem. He was no longer the weedy Yid of our school-days; instead he moved through the city with self-confident ease. A man among men, a real Yiddisher *mensh*. One night after a street-corner supper of felafel we all went to the cinema in Zion Square. The first feature was a film about the Six-Day War, made up cheaply from bits of old newsreel. It was received with wild enthusiasm. Though it is difficult to credit today the audience cheered every time Mosche Dayan or Itzak Rabin appeared on the screen. Unfortunately the main feature was less to their liking; the story of a man destroyed by Stalinism, fiction based on fact. The audience quickly lost interest, and only perked up when the unlucky victim was accused of being a Zionist. Finally, as the man looked through his prison bars toward the sky, someone shouted,

"He's expecting the Israeli airforce to come and rescue him!"

Everybody laughed. As we were leaving Linda, unable to restrain herself, started yelling at a bunch of the yahoos.

"What is the matter with you," she cried, "don't you have any respect for suffering?"

"*Ma zeh?*" they said, tapping their foreheads. Then Linda, out of control, spat in their faces. This caused them to forget their good humour; they swore at Linda, they called her a whore. They gathered their empty Coca-Cola bottles and flung them at us; and as the glass shattered on the concrete floor they began to close in. Four Esaus, looking for a fight. What sort of joke is this, I thought, to be beaten up in Israel by fellow Jews? With a single movement Solomon grabbed the leader, clutched him and positioned him; then with a graceful gesture cast him over his shoulder. The unsuspecting partner of this pas de deux performed a somersault in the air and crashed on to the floor. His hairy brethren rushed Solomon, but it was a half-hearted attack, and Solomon danced amongst them till they all fell dizzily to the ground, like the walls of Jericho.

"Where did you learn to fight like that?" I asked.

"In the army," said Solomon, "I was the lightweight wrestling champion."

He invited us to feel his biceps, "You know what," he said, "whenever I fight someone I still imagine I'm hitting Beaky, that anti-semitic bastard."

"But they were Jews you beat up tonight, Solomon," I said. "Only Yemenite Jews," he said, "it's all they understand."

So even in a nation of Jews there were still *yoks*.

Next thing we heard about Solomon was that he'd been chosen to represent Israel at the Munich Olympics. Quite an achievement for Solomon, the boy who hated games. We watched the opening ceremony on Solomon's mother's colour television; you should have seen her *kvell* as her only son marched past behind the Israeli flag. I'll swear her chest swelled out a good six inches. Poor woman, it was her last bit of pleasure.

Solomon did moderately well in his competition, though he did not win a medal; but he had his day of fame, none the less. He was probably sleeping when the Black September terrorists burst into the Israeli athletes' quarters. All through that day we sat in front of the television set seeing nothing but those white walls and the gunmen on the balcony in the balaclava helmets, hearing nothing but banalities from sports commentators unaccustomed to dealing with such events. We knew that Solomon was inside. What could he be thinking? Deeper than the politics of the Middle East was he tormented by a single thought? That Beaky was having the last laugh. Solomon could not wrestle with men holding machine-guns; his skills were trumped, he was as helpless as a schoolboy again. When darkness fell we saw the coaches fill, ready to take the terrorists and their hostages to the airfield outside Munich. Linda swore that she could make out the features of Solomon, but all their faces looked the same to me. Written on them all was the awful realisation that whatever they did the Jews were doomed to lose out; you learn to fight to defend yourself against the yoks and — what happens? — they get guns and shoot you instead. One of the athletes looked back on the steps of the coach — perhaps that was Solomon — and held out his hands as if to say, what more can we do? Then at midnight came the surprise news. There had been a shoot-out at the airfield. All the hostages were safe. The terrorists were dead.

"Thank God for that," said Linda.

The *Daily Mirror* was sticking through our letter-box next morning, like a dagger in a corpse. The headline screamed: THE TRAGIC BLUNDER. It seemed that the German police had made a "tragic blunder" in announcing the results of the shoot-out; they got it the wrong way round; it was the athletes who were wiped out, not the terrorists.

I began to shiver as the information sank in. Solomon was dead! I recalled with what pride he showed us his biceps that night in Jerusalem; but all the training was gone for nothing now. Solomon was dead. Linda cried all day, she cursed the Palestinians. But I could not see it like that, to me the Palestinians were instruments of fate, Solomon's inevitable nemesis; it was merely a cruel irony that this particular death struggle should be between two semitic peoples. Out of habit I turned to the sports section of the newspaper. But what I saw turned me cold. "Queens Park Rangers went hurtling out of the League Cup," I read, "following two tragic blunders by Rangers defender Ian Evans." It had been quite a night for tragic blunders! The carelessness of some sub-editor had equated the two events, the terrible with the trivial; or perhaps it did really reflect how others saw the Munich Massacre. As a good away win for the Palestinians. It was, indeed, confirmation of Beaky's final triumph.

All this happened a few years ago, already. Since then the news has not been too good; nothing seems to have gone right since the Yom Kippur War. They have even built a mosque in Regents Park. Last week I met the Prince of Shmattes in the street. Only he isn't so clever any more, these days he has to wear his own *shmattes*. People stopped buying his suits and the economic crisis finished him off. He was on his way to the post office to collect his pension. Solomon's mother never recovered from the shock, and was senile before she was sixty. Now every young man who visits she thinks is her son, me included. And I go along with the pretence. What harm in that? My parents keep nagging me to give them a grandchild. But I want any child of mine to be born in Israel. *L'shanah haba-ah birushalayim.* Next year in Jerusalem.

THE LUFTMENSH

What is Joshua Smolinsky, private eye, doing in Philip Roth's former room at a colony for writers? In New England, no less.

The answer begins, as do most things in my life, with a knock on my office door. He held the door open so long that the room filled with the stale air that passes for atmosphere in Los Angeles.

"Do you recognise me?" said my visitor.

"No," I said, "should I?"

"Such short memories," he whispered. "Once I was famous."

"Sorry," I said.

"It doesn't matter," he said, "I'm nothing but a hack now."

"Sit down," I said, "you look like a ghost."

His face turned from white to green. "That's just what I am," he said, "not a ghost, but a ghost-writer."

"Smolinsky," I cried, "that's who!" A string of scandalous best-sellers, much praised by critics, then silence, only noted by me because of the coincidence in names.

"Tell me," he said, "what is the worst thing that can happen to a writer?"

"Run out of ideas?" I said.

"No, no, no," he said, "it's far worse to lose your voice. To know that your ideas are not your own. That's what has happened to me. Every thought in my head belongs to Victor."

"Who?"

"Victor Stenzil, the Yiddish writer," he said. "I have been chosen to ghost his life story."

"Never heard of him," I said. "Is he still alive?"

"I don't know," he said, "that's what I want you to discover."

"Need an ending for your book?" I said.

He didn't laugh. "If he is still alive there is hope," he said, "perhaps he will release me from the contract. But if he is dead

I am doomed to be his ghost for as long as I live. Please find him!"

"Where do I start?" I said.

"The colony," he said.

"In the beginning," said my client, "it was wonderful at the colony. Each day a whole day of uninterrupted writing. No distractions; no visitors, no newspapers, no television. There were eight of us in residence. We lived as a community, and naturally we had rules. We took breakfast and dinner together in a communal dining-room, but between times we were expected to stay in our rooms and write. Of course conversation at table was lively; work-in-progress was read out to loud cheers and jeers; sometimes we got drunk. Once or twice women were obtained. Yes, everything was going swimmingly until the ninth guest arrived. Victor! What a sight! His hair looked like a hundred invisible hands were trying to tug it from his scalp. Meanwhile, other hands shoved tufts into his ears and up his nose. And what a nose! It hung between his eyes like a giant tear-drop. He introduced himself by reading a poem. Not even one of his own.

> 'I should have died with you,
> But I found dying too hard.
> Now I do everything to hide with colour
> The convulsions of my body and word.
>
> Neither grief nor anger can drown
> The guilt of my living on,
> My guilt because the flames of Treblinka
> Didn't consume me flesh and bone.'

We received it in silence. It was not the sort of poem you could cheer. 'That's by Halper Leivick,' he said, 'I don't suppose you boys have ever heard of him. Am I right?' Night after night Victor went on, dominating our conversation, till we began to dread the evening meal. Eventually, rather than listen to him every evening, we began to sneak into town for supper."

"So what happened?" I said.

"Victor broke the rules," he said, "he knocked on my door in writing-time. From that moment I have not written a word of my own. 'I have chosen you,' he said. 'For what?' I said. 'I want you to tell the story of my life,' he said. 'You are a writer,' I said, 'tell it yourself.' 'I cannot, I am cursed,' he said, 'I am a wanderer, always a wanderer.' As we spoke in my doorway streamers of breath floated from our mouths, mingled, and became a single cloud. 'Listen to me,' said Victor, 'it is my tragedy that the Nazis never reached New York. You think I am crazy? Perhaps. But look at me. What am I? A *luftmensh*. A man of air. Without substance. Possessed by history. Full of dreams and nightmares. All the war I was safe. Until the first survivors arrived from Europe. Oy, the guilt I felt then! I was ashamed. Come summer I wouldn't roll up my shirt-sleeves in case someone saw that I had no number on my arm. The mark of Abel! Because I was not a victim I felt like a murderer. I wanted to explain my guilt to you all. But no, what did you do? You ran away to your tootsies in town. Now you will not escape so easily.' 'Why me?' I said. 'Choose someone else.' But the next day a contract arrived from my agent. Which I signed. Don't ask me why. The fact is that Victor grew, in the space of a single day, from an object of irritation into a living obsession. He became my subject, and I his."

"But where do you get all the facts from?" I said.

"That's the point," he said, "I am inventing his life. And I cannot stop. That's what's driving me mad!"

"So where was Victor last seen?"

"At the colony," he said. "He vanished that night. Without trace. Leaving all his things in his room."

A beautiful fall day. Just cold enough to see the breath float from your body and drift through the still air like ectoplasm. A single hermit thrush sat singing on the picket fence; flute-like notes of joy, chucks of lamentation and a scolding *tuk-tuk-tuk*. All in the same song. The leaves blazed on the trees like fragments from an exploded patchwork quilt. New England! I checked into the colony as "Smolinsky". The girl at reception didn't know one Smolinsky from another. Nor did my fellow writers. There is only one difference between writers and detectives; writers invent plots whereas detectives discover them. And pretty soon my

comrades were plotting against me. They wanted to know why I
never contributed anything to the work-in-progress soirées. So
they bribed a call-girl to rob me. I watched as she crept from the
bed to the desk and began to search in vain for the booty. My
anger mingled with desire as her body grew luminous in the
moonlight; but it was business before pleasure, and in a moment
I had her spreadeagled on the floor, a collection of movable parts,
which soon confessed its crime. After that incident my colleagues
lost patience and began abusing me behind my back.

"You know how he made it, don't you?" said one. "Thanks to
the Jewish literary mafia. They look after their own." He wasn't
really talking about me, he meant the other Smolinsky, but I
became enraged anyway. I challenged him to a boxing match
and gave him a bloody nose. This conduct was not considered
becoming from a writer. A Jewish one to boot! Therefore I was
expelled from the colony. But I had got what I had come for.
I knew what had happened to Victor's belongings.

The red barn stood amid fields of fresh snow, like a bloodstain on
a sheet. It was crowded with objects for the auction. Victor's
property was Lot 100. In the meantime I nosed around a bit.
Maybe it's because I'm a detective, but the place depressed me.
In every bundle I could see finished lives. A chest full of precision
tools, minute screwdrivers, pointed pincers, and tins, each containing a selection of watch parts; one tin for faces, another for
hands, others for glasses, cases, mainsprings and all the para-
phernalia from which we assemble time. So the local watchmaker
had shuffled off the mortal coil, that was obvious. But I also knew
what tobacco he smoked, what chocolates he liked, what pastilles
he favoured for coughs, colds, sore throats, that he suffered indigestion for many years. No magic, I just read the labels on the
tins. Lot 100 cost me five dollars. It consisted of a shaving-brush,
a pair of old pants and two paperback books. One was a phrase
book entitled *Say It In Yiddish,* the other was *A Streetcar Named
Desire* by Tennessee Williams. The first amused me with its sec-
tions on how to deal with Customs and Passport Control; the
new arrival was advised to say, *"Awt iz min pahs. Voo iz dehr
tsawl-ahmt?"* meaning: "This is my passport. Where is the customs?" I ask you, what country is this where Yiddish is the spoken

language? A country of displaced persons and ghosts, not marked on any map. Victor's Utopia. An insight into his aspirations, but no use in pinpointing his whereabouts. However, the second book provided a clue. Victor had marked the first line of the epigraph, "And so it was I entered the broken world." And had written alongside Stanley Kowalski's name in the cast list, "A real anti-semitic Polak, that's what I need."

"He wants to be a martyr," said Smolinsky.

"So does our driver," I said. He drove the Greyhound like the devil was on his tail under the influence of the rhythms of the red-neck music that he played on his radio. And the further south we went the more reckless he became, jostling with the beat-up cars that criss-crossed our path like headless chicken. As we approached Nashville his mood changed. He calmed down, kept to his lane, and turned off the radio right in the middle of "D-I-V-O-R-C-E". Instead his voice issued from the speakers.

"Ladies and gentlemen," he said, "Nashville has one of the densest concentrations of millionaires in the nation. It is the Athens of the South, location of numerous colleges and universities, and site of the Parthenon, considered the finest example of classic Greek architecture and generally conceded to be the most beautiful building ever constructed. It is on your right now."

And it was! The whole thing reconstructed on a green hill in Nashville, Tennessee. Representing the South's self-image, as a reflection of that former perfect society, also founded upon slavery. Our bus gathered speed again along the backroads where billboards posted by John Birchers demanded, "Get the US out of the UN". Where signs riddled with bullet holes read, "It is Illegal to Shoot on Highways". Dogs strayed beside the road, and every few miles we passed the body of another mashed into the dust by a careless car; sometimes huge black birds stooped over the corpse like mourners. One lifted its face to reveal the curved beak and naked head of a vulture. A pick-up truck flashed by at a crazy speed leaving the impression of the contents of its open back; two blonde boys in dungarees sitting beside a stiffening deer. The land was flat and full of swollen rivers. Wide areas were flooded and deserted save for dead trees that protruded from the water like dislocated limbs.

"The land, like my life," said Smolinsky, "is out of joint."

We cut across the narrow neck where Lake Pontchartrain filters into the Gulf of Mexico and entered New Orleans. We left the Greyhound near Canal Street and stolled into the Vieux Carré, sensing that tropical hint of violence in the quotidian. A black man dressed in top hat and midnight-blue suit rattled past in the cab of a horse and carriage. His white passengers in the rear craned their necks to catch his commentary. His melancholy face, with its statuesque features, was impassive. But I could read his mind. It was filled with terrible dreams of revenge, of revolution, of white necks bared for the guillotine.

Her elbows resting on the bar of the Bourbon Street club, the whore said to her client: "Sometimes, sometimes I look at myself and wonder where my life has gone." A talking blues, dependent not upon inner feeling but on the quality of performance; and this girl with her sfumato cadences and innocent eyes was a performer and a half.

In the background a naked girl swung back and forth beneath a giant clock. A living pendulum. At about nine-thirty the jazz band arrived. Old black men who carefully placed their jackets on hangers and patted out the creases. There were no long solos because their lungs were too worn out to sustain the effort; unlike the whore the feeling was there but the performers were weary. As each musician took a few choruses on his own the rest watched and smiled; some stomped their feet, others just sat as though hypnotised by the sound. An elegy for a messiah who never showed. And who is no longer expected. The music expressed those hopes, and its dying revealed their disillusion. I looked around. Only one black in the audience. And an out-of-towner, judging by the Kodak instamatic hanging from her wrist. Thus will the message be carried to the people, as a silent photograph! Old-time jazz does not appeal to young blacks, it reeks of bondage; they shun it like Israelis ignore their Yiddish heritage. At which point, as if in response to my cue, Victor walked out from the wings and joined the band on stage.

"So the old *meshuggener* is still alive," said Smolinsky, "how did you find him?"

"No problem," I said, "I bought 'This Week in New Orleans'."

The pianist played a twelve-bar blues and Victor began his monologue.

"Which would you rather be," he began, "a warder in a concentration camp or a prisoner? A Cain or an Abel? Let me tell you people something. I used to thank God for the holocaust. You want to know why? I'll tell you for nothing. Because it gave us Jews the right to sit in judgement on this stinking world. But now I am not sure. Why? On account of Israel, that's why. In our own country we Jews are also not perfect. Now answer my question! Cain or Abel? One or the other!"

But before anyone could open their mouths the club was suddenly invaded by a group of black dudes in white zoot suits and young whites in denim duds. They shooed the old musicians from the rostrum and set up their own instruments. "The revolution has come," they announced, "the old order giveth way to the new."

Then a member of the combo began to play the bongos while another in an Afro fright-wig chanted,

> "Jew-Land, On a summer afternoon
> Really, Couldn't kill the Jews too soon
> Now dig. The Jews have stolen our bread
> Their filthy women tricked our men into bed
> So I won't rest until the Jews are dead."

"Over here, you black Nazi!" yelled Victor. "Make a start with me." And he ran up to the singer and spat in his face. Was Victor going to become a martyr at last, in this seedy bar in New Orleans? "Come on, you *shvartzer*, show us what a *mensh* you are," he shouted, "stick a knife in my old heart."

The naked girl swung to and fro below the clock, Victor's spittle rolled down the black man's cheek, and we all stood in silence. But it isn't always that easy to get killed, even in New Orleans.

"Shit, I don't want to hurt you, old man," said the singer, "I didn't mean the words literally. Personally, I like the Jews. I'm just sick and tired of hearing how the Jews suffered. Man, you're hogs for punishment. Let someone else get a word in. Shit, we've suffered as much."

"In that case, young man," said Victor, "you'd better improve your script. Find yourself a writer!"

"Why aren't you back at your desk?" said Victor.

"I want to break the contract," said Smolinsky, "I've had enough."

"A contract is a contract," said Victor, "you gave your word."

"Well, at least stay in one place," said Smolinsky, "so we can get it over with as quick as possible."

"I told you," said Victor, "I'm a wanderer."

"Then I'll wander with you," said Smolinsky, "till the book is finished."

"This trip could be dangerous," said Victor. "I've heard rumours of a plantation near the Mississippi state line that still keeps slaves. I intend to find it."

The old bullshitter!

"Pardon me, gentlemen," said a city slicker who had been listening in, "but I've got a little tale that might interest you. About how I nearly shot a man. Well, this guy pulls up his truck just beside where me and Curtis are loading our guns for a duck-shoot and reaches for his glove compartment — you know, it's kinda sad that nowadays you're so suspicious of everyone — but I can see that Curtis is thinking the same thing, and in a second we've both levelled our guns at the guy. If he'd had a gun in there we'd have shot him in half before he could have twitched. Want to know what was in there? A dead duck. 'Is this yours?' says he. Gentlemen, the moral is plain. It ain't safe to poke your nose into other folks' affairs. Even if your intentions are honourable."

"What was that all about?" said Smolinsky.

I said I would stick with them for a while. My conduct was unprofessional, but I wanted to keep an eye on my namesake.

North of New Orleans Victor got caught by a cop pissing in the Mississippi. "What the hell do you think you're doing?" the cop called out of his car window.

"Forgive me, officer," said Victor, "but these days my bladder has no resistance."

"Come over here," said the cop. Victor hesitated. "Don't worry," said the cop, "I'm not going to bite you." So Victor approached the battered black and white car. "You're not from round here, are you?" said the cop.

"Correct," said Victor, "I'm from a village near Warsaw, in Poland." "No kidding," said the cop, "I was there during the war. Tell you what I remember most about the place. The goats' milk. Used to have it delivered to the camp every morning by an old woman. Till the Russians took control and we were sent packing. I often wonder what became of that old peasant and her goats. I can tell you, I was real sorry when Poland went communist. Believe me, I thank God I'm an American. Though not quite so often since Nixon's fucking caper. And then that Ford. Who did he give us for Vice-President? A billionaire who didn't know shit about us poor folks. Listen, if you say you've got a weak bladder I can understand that, because my bladder's weak too, but what can a man who was born rich know about poverty, tell me that? What we need in the White House is a farmer from around here who was raised in dirt. Now off you go, and try not to pee in your pants."

"A man after my own heart," said Victor as we tramped north-wards over the rolling lands that seemed to take their rhythm from the river.

"Have you boys ever tasted goats' milk?" asked Victor. "That's real milk. Milk that don't taste like water. Chock full of fatty globules and flocculent curds. My aunt used to sell the stuff. In the old country."

We were sitting drinking beer in the warm winter sun by the banks of the Mississippi.

"My father was a rabbi in a *shtetl* outside Warsaw," said Victor, "and my mother was also descended from rabbis. Much good that did either of them when the defeated Russian army passed through the town. After the pogrom I was taken in by my Aunt Zelda. She was a spinster. Made her living from goats. Sold milk and cheese from a little stall in the market square. My job was to milk the goats every morning before *cheder*. I've never been happier. Sitting on the three-legged stool squeezing the milk into my bucket. As a rule Aunt Zelda left me alone with the goats except on those mornings when the nannies were especially fidgety, then she would come down with me and lock away all the billies. This was in accordance with an injunction she had found in the *Shulchan Aruch*, the Code of Jewish Law; namely,

'One should not look when either animals, beasts, or fowl have intercourse.' In response to my enquiries concerning this behaviour she quoted, 'The thought of fornication only comes into a mind devoid of wisdom. So stop asking questions, go to *cheder* and learn.' Being a spinster Aunt Zelda had peculiar ideas about sex, which she revealed to me soon after my *bar-mitzvah*. She informed me that my private parts had been given me by God so that I might know when the devil was filling my mind with evil thoughts. At which point my penis would grow hard. 'One is forbidden to willingly harden himself or to bring to himself the thought about women,' she quoted. If this should occur, God forbid, I must open the *Torah* and save myself with holy thoughts. One morning, to illustrate what would happen to me if I gave in to temptation she let the billy-goats loose and made me watch their junketings astride the nannies. Afterwards she showed me their eyes. 'Look at those pupils,' she said, 'slanted like the devil's.' Despite the warnings I could not control my dreams. At night the devil appeared in the guise of voluptuous females until I succumbed and stained my sheets. Naturally Zelda was horrified at the sight. So many lamentations you would have thought Jerusalem had fallen. Fortunately the *Shulchan Aruch* had an appropriate passage. 'A man should be very careful to avoid hardening himself,' she read, 'therefore it is forbidden to sleep on one's back with his face upward, or to sleep with his face downward, but to sleep on his side, in order not to come to hardening himself.' Thereafter I suffered dreadfully from insomnia, fearing to drop off in a proscribed position."

"Carry on," said Smolinsky. He was joyfully copying down every word.

"Despite my aunt I got a bit of an education," continued Victor, "thanks to the *mocher seforim*, the book pedlars, who passed through from time to time and always stopped for a glass of milk and a gossip. They told me stories of the world outside the *shtetl*. For instance, I learned how students in Germany were burning all books written by Jews. And I didn't even know that Jews were allowed to write books! I became the best customer of the *mocher seforim*. I swallowed every word I read, just as I had swallowed Aunt Zelda's teachings. And when I discovered how she had misled me I hated her. Instead of fasting on *Yom Kippur* I went to dances and ate pork. Then one day, without a word, I left for America. The Nazis were in power in Germany and I knew what they had planned for the Jews. I took what Hitler said literally. You see what I am saying? I left Zelda behind on purpose. I didn't try to persuade her to come with me. I condemned her to Treblinka! Now do you understand my guilt? Enough!"

Near St Francisville we happened upon a plantation house shining out from within a grove of live oak and crape myrtle bearded with Spanish moss, its jalousied galleries and colonnaded balconies back-lit by the cascading light. The place appeared to be haunted by a Southern belle who beckoned us inside.

"Would you care for the tour?" she said.

"Why not?" said Victor.

"The house has been restored," she said, "by the combined forces of the Daughters of the American Revolution and the National Society of the Colonial Dames of America. This lady here was our inspiration." She pointed to a pen-and-ink portrait framed on the wall. "Miss Eliza Pirrie. The young lady of the house when it was at the height of its glory. She was a pretty thing, don't you think? Many people see a resemblance to Julie Nixon."

On the road again. "History never repeats itself," said Victor, "but I wouldn't be surprised to see another Nixon in the White House. Julie, this time. Swept to power by the Nixons, the Eisenhowers and the followers of a resurrected Eliza Pirrie. Mark my words."

"That's my job," said Smolinsky.

There was an isolated plantation six miles below the Louisiana-Mississippi state line. Across a railway track, rusty with lack of use, down a bumpy unpaved road, over a wooden bridge and there was the rambling plantation house. A fading notice read, "Accommodation". We knocked. There was shouting within, then a boy emerged, his teeth in braces.

"What do you want?" he said.

"A room," we said.

"Follow me," he said. He led us through a gate at the side of the house, to where a second gallery ran off at right angles. He opened one of the doors in this gallery. Inside was a grand room with oak panels, old prints on the walls and lead-light windows with wooden shutters.

"Look through the windows," said Victor, "see how their panes distort everything. That's because the slaves who had to make them couldn't produce perfect glass."

"You like the room?" said the kid.

"Magnificent," said Victor, "just what we were looking for. You'll be able to work here all right, eh, Smolinsky?"

So the kid left us. Because he was not suspicious of us I became suspicious of him. Why no registration? No payment in advance? No number on the door? And no key? But Victor was more interested in a ledger laid open on the desk. It contained an inventory of the slaves. All neatly displayed. Column one, name; column two, age, weight and brief description; column three, price; column four, present value.

"Look at the date," cried Victor, "this book is still being used!"

The sky was stained red where it touched the land. The winter silhouetttes of the trees lurked like moving creatures. We sat on our porch watching the darkness fall. There was no denying the edgy fascination of the place. Indeed, it was this vaguely dangerous charm that made it so sensational. Everything seemed magnified; the house, our isolation, the moon as it rose. Pale nocturnal creatures snuffed the ground, owls hooted. Slowly the sky sucked up the moon. Until it shone so brightly that all the buildings on the plantation began to glow; and even the distant slave quarters glimmered.

"It was one family per hut," said Victor, "didn't matter if there were two or twenty in the family."

Suddenly screams filled the air. Real blood-curdling screams! My perception went into overdrive. I began to imagine impossible things. The trees seemed to be creeping closer. New sounds. Not imagination. The chink of metal on metal. Through the night I saw the shimmer of chains in motion. Moving towards us. And then as if being formed out of the darkness itself there emerged a huge Negro. Naked except for the chains around his ankles. It was as though the past had come to life.

"It can't be a ghost!" hissed Smolinsky.

"No way," I said. "Ghosts don't bleed."

"What is your name?" said Victor.

"Abel," replied the slave.

Then two more faces floated out of the darkness like white balloons. It could almost have been a party for there were orange flashes and bangs. Except they were guns going off. And the game, as the man in the club had warned us, was kill the intruders. So we ran like rabbits. But Abel slowed us down, with his chains and his wounds. And they caught us by the deserted road.

"Thank your friends, nigger," they said, "on account of them we're going to kill you."

They would have, too, if Victor hadn't stepped in the way and got shot instead.

"Don't die!" begged Smolinsky.

Victor was groaning in the dirt, bleeding to death. Abel was gasping for breath. Me and Smolinsky were petrified. Awaiting our turn in front of the firing squad. When in the distance we all saw the blue lights of the Highway Patrol. As a rule I don't expect much from cops. But our saviour just happened to be Victor's fellow capriphile. So Victor lived. What's more he persuaded those southern cops that a plantation worked by slaves was operating under their noses. The slaves were freed. Smolinsky's contract was cancelled. And Victor was a hero. He played all the clubs with a bandage wrapped around his head. With his new partner. They called themselves "Cain & Abel".

"Once we were slaves," they said, "but now we are free. As free as air!"

Smolinsky, on the other hand, is learning Yiddish.

THE EVOLUTION OF
THE JEWS

"Remember you are a Jew," my father said when I was old enough to stand on my own four feet. As if the anti-semites would let me forget! They have been killing Jews in the miombo ever since the drought began. Before that there were pogroms in the nyika to the east. Now they have my scent. And I am in danger. They came upon us during our old-fashioned mating rituals. You'd think the rabbis would relax some of the rules at a time like this. But no. "We must obey God's commandments," they say. So we males have got to knock ourselves silly with the head-slamming competition. And after that, if we're still capable, we're expected to nibble the rear end of a female so that she wees into our mouth. The odours are supposed to suffuse our olfactory membranes to let us know whether the lady's on heat or not, but between you and me I spit the stuff out as quick as I can. Personally, I'd much rather just give the girl a nudge in the backside, and if she's not interested she can walk off. But there's no arguing against tradition. Just my luck this afternoon I got a real athlete. A dozen times in four hours she made me perform. Then the lookouts spotted the lions. Two of the brutes. Moving in our direction. "Run!" they signalled. Fat chance!

You're probably wondering what a community of Jews is doing living in the African savanna. Well, we're the lost tribe. How do I know? My father told me. What proof can I give? For starters, there's the statue of Moses wearing horns. Just like mine. Put the rest down to evolution. If every other creature in the world wanted to do you in you'd also head for the lowlands and grow a long neck. And four legs are faster than two. I know a long neck is a life-saver, but sometimes I think of it as a curse. Because all animals are our enemies and because we can see them coming with our long necks we spend all day watching for them. We don't relax for a minute. What sort of life is that? We stand still for hours grazing on the tree-tops. Then we ruminate. Chewing over our food again and again, chewing over our worries also, belching all the while. The only problem we Jews have been spared is indigestion. All in all we are pessimistic creatures. With a tendency to melancholia. To raise our spirits we say that while our feet stand in shit our heads are in the clouds. Believe it or not, that daft saying got us into our present difficulties.

When the rains did not come, we knew we would be blamed. We were blamed for the floods. Why not the drought? During the floods the stupider animals begged us to eat the clouds. We laughed. So they killed us. The floods subsided. Now we are accused of stealing the clouds. Let me quote a typical anti-semitic libel. "They say their heads are in the clouds," it goes, "so they must know where they have gone. Friends, the Jews have stolen our clouds!" We are accused of being alien, aloof, stiff-necked. And worse. "If it were not for the Jews," runs another libel, "there would be no problems. Neither floods. Nor droughts." To be rid of such problems forever they decide to wipe out the Jews. Which explains my predicament. Hunted by lions.

They have found me. I can hear the snuffing of their snouts. Their excited gurgles and growls. I can smell the stale blood on their disgusting breath. It will be an ignominious death, to be ripped apart by such obnoxious beasts. I retreat slowly, backing away. My hoofs carefully testing the ground. Suddenly one of my back legs slips, for I have reached an escarpment, and in a panic I all but tumble over. For an instant I am more frightened of falling than of the lions. I remember the unfortunate fate of one of my uncles who stepped backwards while browsing at a tree by the edge of a drop and found no ground beneath his feet. His neck caught in a fork between branches and he hung choking, twenty inches of tongue hanging out of his mouth buzzing with flies. When we discovered him lions were already feeding from his hind legs. Ugh! Since that day I have been terrified of falling. It has become a phobia. Indeed when I see my reflection in a water-hole it seems a miracle that such a creature can stand at all. Trapped. There can be no escape on account of the escarpment. Lions leap. I turn and kick out with my heels. I catch the first lion in the belly and it rolls over grunting. But the second lands on my back. I try to shake the brute off but its claws are in my flanks. Forgetting that I stand on the brink of an escarpment, I gallop forward, the lion still riding on my back. The slope is so steep that we reach a dizzying speed and the lion is now hanging on, not to kill me, but to save its own skin. I am safe. So long as I do not stop. But then above the thunder of my hoofs I hear a deeper rumble from the heavens. And I feel rain upon my muzzle. What *mazel*! The lion springs off my back leaving long raking scars — the butcher — and runs around catching raindrops on its tongue. The drought is over. God be praised. The Jews will live a few more days.

What else can I tell you about us? That we are big-hearted is well known. We need big hearts to pump the blood all the way up to our heads. Which are not so big. Our diet is strictly controlled. We are permited to eat only fruit that grows on trees; all food from the ground is forbidden as unclean. "If God had wanted us to eat dirt," the rabbis say, "He would have given us short necks like pigs." So day after day we chew mimosa and prickly acacia, though my papillae cry out for variety. We sleep very little, no more than a few minutes at a time. Which is just as well, as far as I am concerned, for no sooner do I shut my eyes than I am visited with the most terrifying nightmares. I dream of death in all its varieties: by tooth, by claw, by drought, by flood, by disease, by fire. I dream of pogroms, of massacres, of trials, of tortures. I hear the cruel laughter of anti-semites. But the nightmare that frightens me the most is the shortest. I dream that I fall. And cannot get up. At which point, of course, I awaken and climb to my feet. Neck. Backwards. Forwards. On to knees. Neck. Hind legs. Neck again. Stretch. A shake of the tail.

All is quiet in the miombo. There is neither flood nor drought. Everything is growing according to its season. Except for the odd outbreak of anti-semitism we are left alone. We know that it cannot last. The peace. But we try to make the most of it. Our neck muscles begin to feel like elastic rather than rods of iron. In short, we relax. One day in search of a more arcane variety of acacia I wander off alone, far away from my fellow Jews. Following an unfamiliar path my eye is attracted by a glimmer in the grass. I look down upon a row of brightly-coloured fruits stretching as far as I can see. Which is a long way. I am tempted. And against my better judgement I begin to follow this trail of fruit. The aroma that wafts up as some squash beneath my hoofs convinces me that they will taste better than anything I have eaten before. Until at last I can resist the temptation no longer. I bend my neck and take a step forward, my tongue tingling in anticipation of the forbidden fruit, and walk straight into the pit. The ground gives way beneath my feet and I fall among a shower of branches and brightly coloured fruit into a deep hole. I am buried alive. Only my head is above ground. A nightmare come true! It is a miracle that I do not have a heart attack.

I curse myself for my greed. For my carelessness. Why did I forget that Jews are never safe? That behind every gift lurks danger? That for every pleasure comes a punishment? I would cry out. But for screams you need vocal chords, which we Jews have not got. And you cannot *whisper* for help! So I must await my fate. At least I am not dead.

I wait all day. Then as the sun sinks strange creatures approach. My instinct is to run, but I cannot move. So I try to scare them. I stretch out my neck until my head is horizontal, my ears spread stiffly, my nostrils flaring, my eyes blazing. But my captors do not run away. Instead they continue their entry out of the sun. And when I finally recognise them I really do have a heart attack, anyway the blood rushes from my head and I almost faint. For these creatures walk upon two legs and have short necks just as we Jews once had. I have fallen into the clutches of the worst anti-semites of them all. Men! And they are going to lynch me. One of the murderers has a pole with a noose attached. They toss the loop over my head and as it tightens I feel the rope bite into my neck. Knowing the end is near I begin to recite, "*Shema yisroel. . . .*" Then everything goes black.

It goes black because they have thrown a blanket over my head. Thus blinded and trussed, I am dragged from my trap like Samson among the Philistines. Again my heart stops pumping. I swoon. And one of my tormentors cries out, "Ma zeh?" I recognise the language. *Ma.* What. *Zeh.* Is this? Hebrew! So Hebrew is still spoken in the world. Oh, irony of ironies. I have been kidnapped by Jews. Unevolved, original Jews. I try to communicate with them the lost tribe has been found, but it is no use; my neck too long, my voice too low. Or else they do not know Yiddish. However, there is nothing wrong with my hearing. I learn that I am to be transported to the Promised Land. Their country. My country! Which explains why they have not developed like us. What need for a long neck when all men are your brothers? What need for four legs when there is no assassin to flee? I want to explain to my co-religionists that I will gladly go wherever they lead. But I cannot. And so I return to Israel in chains.

But the bondage does not last. I am taken to Jerusalem and released in a park fragrant with mimosa. At first I ask myself, "Why do they not invite me into their homes?" But then I remember my neck and smile. They would have to build tall houses to accommodate me.

How popular I am! Every day scores of parents bring their kids to visit me. They laugh and clap their hands to see such a Jew. I bend my neck to whisper to them. But they do not hear or do not understand. Never mind. We are brothers. What happiness! What security! I am a king in Israel. And all around me, snarling behind bars, are the anti-semites that once lorded it over the miombo. God is in his heaven. But even now in this lovely land — my own country — I cannot stop worrying. What is there to worry about? I'll tell you. The evolution of the Jews. Make no mistake, evolution happens every day. I tremble for the kids. I am frightened by the way the hair forms thick and mane-like upon their heads. By the way their teeth grow sharp, their nails claw-like. And each time I see a Jew carrying a gun I shiver. Because I am reminded of the accursed Sir Samuel Butler — may his memory be blotted out — a Haman who shot Jews for sport. And once tasted our flesh! "When roasted," he gloated, "it is delicious." Even in this park I hear things. Stories of battles. Roars of triumph. Strange words. Uranium. Plutonium. If only I could warn them. Tell them that evolution is the secret weapon of the anti-semites. That evolution is not inevitable. And must be fought. I want to cry, "Do you not see how you are changing?" But in Israel I am dumb.

Jews may change but the laws are eternal. Here also I am only permitted to eat acacia and mimosa. However, I have noticed a tree in the next enclosure which bears orange fruit. When the wind blows right the scent from them prickles my papillae. "Shlomo," I say to myself, "remember what happened last time you were tempted. You almost died." "Ah, but God works in strange ways," I reply, "if I had not fallen into the pit I would not be in Israel now." I decide to see if I can reach the fruit. That will be the test. If God doesn't want me to eat it He will have put it out of reach. So I lean my chest against the fence and stretch out my neck. The orange fruit dangles in between my eyes. Just a few more inches. And then my tongue curls around its tangy skin. But before I can pluck the fruit from the tree the fence collapses beneath my weight and my legs splay outwards. I wave my neck backwards and forwards. But it is hopeless. I cannot get up!

"Shlomo," I say to myself, "you're done for." With such a conclusion you need a bit of consolation. Who likes to die in vain? So I ask myself, "Why has God done this to you?" And I answer, "I have been sent as a warning to Israel. I am dumb, but my fate speaks." I am a prophet!

THE TEXAS STATE
STEAK-EATING CONTEST

The kid was dressed all in black. He looked like he was in mourning for life. Actually it was just for his father, Hammond Hammerhead I, Texas cattle baron, recently deceased.

"I don't think my father's death was an accident," he said, "I think he was murdered."

That was the gist of his opening statement. It was full of flights of fancy but I excused him on account of the fact he'd just returned from a European university. Meanwhile, back at the Hammerhead Ranch things had been happening fast; his Uncle Claude had declared himself boss and likewise taken possession of his widowed sister-in-law, so that poor Hammond Hammerhead II, arriving too late for his father's funeral was just in time for his mother's wedding. Now the kid's mind was full of mayhem; he was convinced that his uncle had bumped off his father and robbed him of his inheritance. But he seemed a bit short on evidence. So I offered a Freudian interpretation of his obsession, mentioning Oedipus by name.

The kid was not impressed. "Listen, shamus, if I want my motives analysed I'll pay a shrink," he snapped back, his European refinement gone west. "You're an investigator, an empiricist, so go and investigate."

"Why come all the way from Amarillo to hire me?" I said. "Aren't there any good detectives in Texas?"

"First, I'm too well-known in Texas; if I was seen within half a mile of a private eye people would know," said the kid. "Second, my uncle owns most of the detectives in Texas, not to mention half the police force. So I came out to Los Angeles and picked the unlikeliest sounding investigator in the book. Who ever heard of a private eye called Joshua Smolinsky?"

I defended my good name, but the kid wasn't interested.

"I'll tell you what, Joshua," he said, "come down to the ranch with me. I'll introduce you as my Professor of Literature. Do you know anything about literature, Joshua?"

The cowboy stood larger-than-life outside the Big Texan Steak Ranch, on a billboard welcoming me to the "Home of the Free 72oz Steak". Obviously an irresistible invitation to freedom-loving Texans, for the place was full of aborigines behaving like no one ever would outside of Texas. The décor was nineteenth-century Texan, with scant respect to verisimilitude, and the staff were "six-gun-toting waitresses", dressed according to anatomy rather than historical accuracy, for each had a skirt up to her *tochis*. We joined a crowd round one of the tables where a gent was actually trying to devour seventy-two ounces of steak: it was only free, of course, if you finished the lot. His progress was watched over by big men in stetsons who shook their heads pessimistically. The headwaiter, identified by his sheriff's star, came over to see how he was doing. By now he was in trouble. "Hey, Sheriff," he said, "do I have to eat baked potato too?"

"You surely do," came the reply. Beside the baked potato four thick steaks sat growing cold. Unkindly, as if to rub in the guy's failure, the head-waiter announced that a fellow in a yellow shirt had just licked up the last of his 72oz dinner. The cowboys trooped off to observe this phenomenon, to memorise his face, for he could be a good bet in the restaurant's upcoming Texas State Championship Steak-Eating Contest. The head-waiter spied Hammond.

"Good to see you again, Mr Hammerhead," he said, "we're hoping for great things from you in this year's contest."

"Not much to beat," said Hammond, "the last winner only managed sixteen pounds in two hours."

A fiddler and a girl country singer emerged caterwauling from the restaurant's obscurity. They cavorted before a pair of quivering carnivores. The fiddler cocked his head to one side and jerked his hand like he was giving himself an upper-cut; at once notes leaped from the screeching catgut. The girl stood her ground, shook her curly brown hair, leaned back and yelled out "D-I-V-O-R-C-E!"

Out came the words, in went the meat. The man at the table fished
in his pocket for some dollar bills, and with a flashing smile
pushed them under the lace garters that both musicians wore on
their arms. A "six-gun-toting waitress" brought more food and
as she put the plates down her bum pointed skywards revealing
red satin and cheap frills. The fiddler produced a cascade of notes
and the couple at the table whooped and stomped. Their plump
legs looked like oil-pumps from the Texas fields as they pounded
up and down.

"That's my Uncle Claude," said Hammond, "the lady with
him's my mother."

"Mother . . . um . . . Uncle, I want you to meet Professor
Joshua Smolinsky," said Hammond. "A Professor of Literature.
Just arrived from Europe." Uncle Claude stared at me. "Harold
Robbins says he is the finest writer in the world," he said, "and I
agree."

Hammond's mother, Gertie, blushed. Her parents had been
Jewish and it showed in her voluptuous lips, her full bosom and
her admiration for professors.

"Professor Smolinsky, please excuse my husband," she said.
"I'm afraid he doesn't have much respect for learning."

"I've nothing against learning 'cept the time it takes," said
Claude. "The world doesn't stand still waiting for you to finish
your education."

I looked at Hammond. But he didn't say a word.

"There's more to university than book-learning," I said just to
fill the silence.

"Why, Professor Smolinsky!" exclaimed Gertie, "you have a
Los Angeles accent."

"I was raised there," I said, "my parents were refugees."
Refugees from New York.

"I was born in Malibu," said Gertie.

"You see what a great country America is?" said Claude.
"What other country turns its refugees into professors? I hope
you are grateful, Professor Smolinsky. You're not a commie are
you?"

"Mother," said Hammond, "I've asked Professor Smolinsky
to spend a few days at the ranch."

The Hammerhead Ranch covered an area about the size of Denmark. Hanging from the bar over the gate, just below the horns and skull of a bull, was a hammer and sickle burned into a piece of wood.

"We had it first," growled Claude, "and I'll be damned if I'd change our brand on account of some commie bastards."

The ranch-house itself was as big as an average castle. Instead of a moat it was surrounded by a swimming pool. On the night before Gertie's second marriage Claude had employed a score of Navajo craftsmen to inlay the walls of the pool with polished turquoise. As the drawbridge was lowered floodlights blazed into life and we were dazzled by scintillas of blue that came shooting from below the water. Except for Claude who was wearing his gold-rimmed shades.

"Oh, Claude," said Gertie, "why didn't you remind me to put on my sunglasses?"

Hammond took me to my room, which was twice the size of my entire Los Angeles apartment. There was a telephone in every corner, and one beside the bed with a tiny screen which showed the face of the caller.

"Tell me again how your father died," I said to Hammond.

"My father was a king among men," said Hammond, "and like a king he loved to entertain. Often he would perform stunts for his guests. His favourite was the Hopi Snake Dance. In which he was partnered by a rattlesnake. Fangless, of course. Naturally his audience was horrified. They assumed the snake was dangerous. Well, on that last occasion they were right. The snake turned on my father and sank its fangs into his tongue. His tongue swelled to the size of a shoe. And he choked to death. The police concluded that my father had been careless. Picked up the wrong snake. An accident. But I know that my father was too sure-footed to do anything so stupid. So someone must have switched the snakes."

"Your Uncle Claude?"

"Who else?"

My room was filled with bells. The telephone. I picked up the receiver beside my bed and Gertie's face appeared on the screen.

"Hello, Professor," she said, "have you everything you need?"

"Thank you, yes," I said.

From the expression on her face I knew that she wanted to tell me something. "Professor Smolinsky, you are Hammond's friend?"

"Yes."

"Did he ever tell you why we sent him to a European university?" she said.

"He hinted."

"So he told you about Olivia?"

"He led me to believe," I said, treading carefully, "that he was sent away because of a girl."

"Nothing more?"

"You must understand, Mrs Hammerhead, that we spoke of such things in terms of literary analogies," I said. "I had to deduce for myself how they related to his life."

Gertie liked that. "Professor Smolinsky," she said, "my husband — that's my late husband — sent Hammond to Europe to get him away from our foreman's daughter." A second figure appeared on the screen. It was Hammond. He was wearing a T-shirt and jockey shorts. Then Gertie put down the receiver and the screen went blank.

I awoke in the middle of the night to find someone in my room. My eyes focused on a grey object that emerged from the shrouds of sleep and took on the features of Claude Hammerhead. "Professor, you look startled," he said, "were you expecting a ghost?"

"What ghost?"

"You tell me." He laughed. "Let's cut out the crap," he said, "are you going to say why you've come to the ranch?"

"Your nephew invited me."

"But why?" He sat down on the end of the bed. "If you want to know, Smolinsky, I don't believe you're a professor," he said, "I figure you're a detective. Hired by my punk of a nephew to find his father's murderer. Am I right?"

"You have a point, Mr Hammerhead," I said, "we Professors of Literature are like detectives in that we must comb texts for clues as to their real meanings."

"Bullshit!" Claude walked to the door. "Ask Hammond what happened to the last private eye who came snooping round here."

Next morning I came face to face with Hammond in the pool.
"Hi, Joshua," he said, "sleep well?"
"Fine," I said, "but you seem to be a family of somnambulists."
"Did someone bother you?"
"I had a visit from your Uncle Claude."
"What did he want?"
"He made an educated guess as to why I'm here."
"You didn't tell him anything?"
I shook my head.
"Hammond, what happened to the first detective you hired?"
"He had an accident."
"What sort of accident?"
"He pulled a gun on a cop."
"But the cop was quicker?"
"That's about it," said Hammond.
"One more thing," I said, "who's Olivia?"
"If you're asking you must know."
"Where is she now?"
"No idea," said Hammond, "after I left she went to join some hippie commune in New Mexico."
"So who might know? Her father?"
"No. Her father's gone. Only Larry."
"Larry?"
"Her brother. He runs a restaurant for freaks in Santa Fe."
"Will you lend me your car?" I said. "I'm thinking of taking a trip to Sante Fe."

Thunder rumbled round the mountains of New Mexico. Torrential rain filled Santa Fe's valley bowl. Lightning flashed till past midnight, lighting up the ghostly peaks. Next morning Santa Fe was as bright as a new pin. Old men sat arguing and nodding on benches in the plaza. A colourful poster pinned to an adobe wall advertised a rodeo with crude pictures of bronco-busters. Indians spread their blankets and displayed their trinkets and fakes on the porch of the ancient Palace of the Governors. Santa Fe was a cosmopolitan mix of Indian architecture, European town-planning and American money.
I stepped of Cerrillos Road into the Golden Temple Natural

Foods Center. It was full of plants and very airy. The waiters and waitresses were soft-spoken, they wore spotless white robes and turbans. I ate gratefully, relieved to know that nothing artificial was descending the oesophagus. A purgatorial meal of avocado, sour cream, cheese and hot peppers; afterwards I cooled off with Golden Ice Cream, also made with natural products.

"Is Larry around?" I asked a waitress. A couple of minutes later a mountain of a man appeared in regulation robes and turban; they suited him like a wedding dress becomes a boxer.

"I'm Larry."

"I'm looking for your sister," I said.

"And who are you?"

"Joshua Smolinsky. *Professor* Joshua Smolinsky."

"Don't mean a thing."

"A friend of Hammond," I said. "He's back in Amarillo."

"That worm," said Larry, "she's better off without him."

"Isn't that for Olivia to decide?"

"A professor, huh?"

"Of literature."

"Okay, Professor," he said suddenly, "I'll take you to her."

We left Santa Fe going northwards over the red Sangre de Cristo mountains, then eastwards through the Rio Grande Gorge toward Taos.

"Does Olivia live in Taos?" I said.

"Not any more," said Larry. "She came up here with her hippie friends after Hammond left her. She was going to join the Indian Pueblo. But the Indians didn't want to know. They had no time for hippies."

We drove through Taos on Kit Carson Road, passing the great scout's house. I'd a soft spot for Kit ever since I'd read the story of his meeting with General Sherman. "I cannot express my surprise," Sherman wrote in a letter, "at beholding a small stoop-shouldered man, with reddish hair, freckled face, soft blue eyes, and nothing to indicate extraordinary courage or daring." That's Joshua Smolinsky, to the life!

Soon we were far into the Carson Forest, climbing high up pine-covered mountains, then turning deeper into the woods at a sign marked "San Cristobel". Larry forced his old Ford Falcon up a steep unpaved road, muddy from the rains, full of boulders and puddles, and as narrow as a bookmark. We continued slowly for seven miles until we reached a small ranch-house built of wood and mud. On the grass within the dooryard were some cones, a broom, several logs, a rusty seat from a tractor, the pelvis of an ox and a wooden box marked "US Mail".

"Olivia's place?" I said. Larry didn't answer. He got out the car and began to walk up a winding path that led eventually to a white building surrounded by trees. It looked like a shrine. There was no sound except for the water dripping from the trees.

"Inside," said Larry.

Olivia wasn't there. Instead there was a big stone which read: "D. H. Lawrence 1885-1930."

"Alrightee, Professor," said Larry, "how's about giving me a lecture on Lawrence in America?"

I gabbed on for a few minutes. But Larry didn't take any notes.

"Thought so," he said, "you're a professor like I'm an Indian guru." I lifted my hands. "Now are you going to tell me what you're really after?"

"I'm a private investigator," I confessed, "Hammond hired me to prove that Claude murdered his father."

"What's that got to do with Olivia?"

"She lived at Hammerhead Ranch," I said, "she may know something."

"And why should she tell you anything?"

"If Claude is guilty," I said, "Hammond will get the ranch."

"So?"

"Olivia will be his wife." In arranging this *shiddach* I was going beyond my brief, but I could see no other way of getting Larry to talk.

"She works in the Visitors Center at the Navajo Tribal Park," he said.

I sped over the great Colorado Plateau aiming to reach Monument Valley before sundown. By late afternoon I was in Utah. Already puffy white mushrooms were growing in the sky, and cloud-bursts criss-crossed the highway as I rushed toward the atomic storms in Hammond's car, feeling as insecure as an insect in the gigantic landscape. Finally I crossed into Navajoland, a separate country in the heart of the continent. Olivia was sitting in the Visitors Center, the only blonde in miles. She was reading a back number of *True Confessions*.

"Hello, Olivia," I said.

She looked up. Her eyes were as bright as the stones in Gertie's swimming pool. "Who are you?"

"Joshua Smolinsky," I said, "I've come from Hammond. He wants to marry you."

She examined me with those blue eyes. "Mr Smolinsky, do you know why Hammond was sent to Europe?"

"I was told it was because of you."

"No, Mr Smolinsky, that wasn't the reason," she said, "he was sent away because he shot my daddy."

Outside the low sun flickered through a layer of boiling, swirling cloud. The earth was like a red sea from which rose the monoliths of Monument Valley, grey going brown beneath a sky as purple as a hot-house grape. The air was full of electric tension, fat drops of rain fell, pitting the sand with as many pinpricks as there were in Olivia's arms.

"It was hushed up," she said, "no one was told. Not even Larry. I knew and the Hammerheads knew. No one else. Except the cops of course."

"But why?"

"Why was he shot? Easy. He saw Hammond fucking his mother."

"Come on." But I remembered what I had seen on that little screen before Gertie had cut us off.

"If you don't believe me," said Olivia, "there's nothing more to say."

There was a tremendous crack of thunder right over us. Then the vision. The final shaft of sunlight struck the furthest monolith and while that flamed against the mauve sky the others began to glow, stronger and stronger, like red-hot coals. The scene flared like a firework, then faded as the sun sank, leaving only the tip of a rainbow as an afterglow between the colourless stones. It was like that tab of truth that sticks to every crime, the tab which I had just begun to feel.

"I believe you."

"You understand why I could never marry Hammond?"

"Yes." Olivia smiled.

"But you still love him?" I said.

"Right first time, Mr S," she said.

"Will you come back with me," I said, "for your father's sake?"

"I'm confused," she said, "I will ask Chief Silena what to do."

"Who?"

Olivia rolled herself another joint. She had been smoking marijuana since early morning when we left the motel in Mexican Hat for the Hopi Reservation. The Hopi had been there undisturbed since the thirteenth century. Their land was so barren no one else wanted it. On the slopes of the mesas were a few artificial fields, irrigated by the midsummer rains, in which grew corn, squash and beans. The mesas jutted out over the plain like the prows of three giant ships; far below the plain looked like a shimmering silver sea. In the distance were the San Francisco Mountains, home of the Hopi gods.

"I really love maps," said Olivia as she navigated, "they are so full of possibilities."

"Like blueprints for a life."

"Hey, Mr Smolinsky, that's good!"

We drove some miles down route 264, then turned off on to a dirt track. In front was an expanse of brown dust, piles of grey rock, clumps of spiky grass; a feverish wind, the slope to the edge of the mesa, the houses of undressed brown stone; beyond a glimpse of the valley below and the dark encircling mountains.

"This is it," said Olivia, "Shongopovi."

It must have been some kind of holiday because Shongopovi was chock-a-block with Hopi.

"Come on," said Olivia.

"If you're sure it's all right."

We trailed down the dusty street towards the houses, all built pueblo-style, each level connected by a wooden ladder. On the topmost roofs golden eagles were chained. They spread their wings to rise on the wind, trying to break free, only to be jerked back again and again by their leg-irons. So what chance would there be for a down-at-heel private eye? We reached the plaza where the crowds were thickest. In the centre a dozen men were standing in a diagonal line, larger-than-life in that confined space. They wore square masks over their faces, kaolin-covered, decorated with a variety of features, feathered head-dresses, capes hanging from their shoulders and brightly-coloured kilts.

"Kachinas," whispered Olivia, "today must be a *niman*."

I didn't understand a word. Brown paper bags were passed along the line. Cobs of corn, melons and oranges were plucked from within and thrown at us, much to the delight of the kids. Suddenly there was silence as the elders of the tribe entered the plaza. The most venerable walked to the head of the fancy-dress parade and began a chant.

"That's Silena, Chief of the Sun Clan," whispered Olivia. "He's thanking the gods for a good harvest." Well, at least no one was starving.

When the ceremony was over Olivia pushed through the crowds to get to her guru.

She was back in a minute. "I'm coming with you," she said.

"What did he say to convince you?" I said.

"To thine own self be true."

"You know, Chief Silena has a theory about Hammerhead's death?" said Olivia as we were approaching Amarillo. "He says the gods killed him. They were angry because he mocked their dance. So they turned the snake upon him and made it potent again."

"It's a theory." Then we passed beneath the hammer and sickle.

The swimming pool looked fine. Except that two of the turquoise stones seemed to be floating toward the surface. Then I saw that they were not stones but eyes, eyes wide open in a white face. Olivia's face. Then there was a shoulder and a breast and a thigh and soon her whole body had broken through the film of water and was floating lifelessly on the surface. She was naked, offering herself to the sky, like a bride on her bed. I pulled her out of the water. She was cold, very cold. Poor Olivia. I covered her.

"Look at her arm," said Claude, "a heroin addict!"

"Suicide," agreed the cops.

"Poor girl," said Claude, "let's call it an accident."

"Another accident," I said.

"What do you mean by that?" said Claude.

I was the only one who attended Olivia's funeral. Larry wasn't told. Hammond was too depressed, he said. But he let me have his car. It was a lonely affair. Returning to the ranch two cars swerved in front, their blue lights flashing, forcing me to stop. Luckily I had emptied the ashtrays. Formerly full of Olivia's roaches. The cops wouldn't have needed another thing.

"Your car?" they said.

They knew it was Hammond's. They knew I was driving. They knew everything.

"Get out."

The only thing they didn't know was that the ashtrays were empty. They pulled them out. Nothing. They were not pleased. They let the air out of the tyres, dragged out the seats, peered into the gas tank and searched under the chassis with flashlights. It was as if they were not human beings at all. In place of heads they wore shiny helmets, in place of eyes they had reflecting shades with black lenses, no hands, just leather gloves; each sported a blue nylon jacket, short and padded, that stopped just above the gun butt. The Hopi saw the Kachinas as messengers from their gods; I wondered what manner of gods these creatures represented.

"O.K., smartass," said one, "where have you hidden it?"

"Hidden what?" I had to be careful. We were beside a busy road, but they could always take me to a quiet spot.

"We had a tip-off," said another, "we know you're carrying dope."

"Why? Need some? Run out at the station?"

"A joker!" said the third as he searched in my stomach for my lunch. I doubled-up, retching.

"That's enough," said number four, "he's had his warning." If they'd hung around they'd have seen that I'd eaten hamburger, french fries and salad with thousand island dressing.

I didn't get undressed. I was expecting visitors. Claude arrived first.

"What do you know?" he said.

"That Hammond murdered Olivia's father," I said.

"Know why?"

"Because he was blackmailing Gertie."

Claude laughed.

"Listen," he said, "Hammond got Olivia's father to switch the snakes. Then he shot him. And went to Europe to wait for the bad news. Unfortunately he didn't reckon on my intervention."

"What about Olivia?"

"Hammond too. She must have found out the real reason for her father's death."

"Very convincing," I said.

"It certainly convinced Larry," said Claude, "in fact he's coming here to have a chat with Hammond." Exit Claude.

Gertie came next.

"Since you arrived here there's been nothing but trouble," she said, "why don't you leave us alone. Go away!"

"And miss the Texas State Steak-Eating Contest? Sorry."

"What do you want of us? Money?"

"I want to know who killed Olivia."

"All right, I did," said Gertie, "she wasn't good enough for my boy. Satisfied?"

"You're joking."

"Professor Smolinsky — or whoever you are," she said, "I would do anything to protect my family." She walked to the door. "You have been warned."

Finally Hammond showed up. My client. "You're not doing very well, are you, Joshua?" he said. "Uncle Claude is still going round murdering people."

"But why should Claude kill Olivia?"

"Because she found out that he paid her father to switch the snakes."

"How?"

"She found a letter."

"A letter?"

"More like a confession."

"So Claude shot her father?"

"Who else?"

Then I told him that Larry was coming down for the Texas State Steak-Eating Contest. Hammond just laughed. The fool.

The Big Texan Steak Ranch was jam-packed for the big night.

The night of the Texas State Championship Steak-Eating Contest. Convoys of "six-gun-toting waitresses" were conveying piles of raw meat to a long trestle table where they dropped them sizzling on to electric hot plates. There was a great deal of whooping and stomping and hollering. Men wearing sashes marked "Judge" were checking their stop-watches. Another man in a striped shirt was writing a list of names on a blackboard with spaces left blank in the "Pounds of Steak Consumed" and "Time Taken" columns. Hammond was the favourite to win, but Larry — a last minute entrant — was the dark horse. There was a gasp and some giggles as Larry took his place at the table next to Hammond, for he was still wearing his outfit from the Golden Temple Natural Foods Center, the turban and the robes.

"Ready, gentlemen?" said a judge.

"Go!" screamed Miss Texas.

Immediately the men at the table bent forward and stuck into their steaks, slobbering meat and juices all over the place. At the end of the first hour Hammond and Larry had each consumed nine pounds of meat. After ninety minutes they were the only two survivors. By the beginning of the third hour Hammond was ready to conceed. But Larry persuaded him to continue. He had no subtle arguments, just a gun.

"Keep eating," he said. Gertie tried to grab Larry, but Claude held her back.

"Our pride is at stake," he said. So we all watched as Hammond ate himself to death. His face took on a purplish hue, like a varicose vein. He could no longer speak, his tongue was too swollen. Then he was gasping for breath, vomiting, bringing up pounds of meat. Finally he sat bolt upright as a spasm passed through his body, and fell forward face down in his plate. Larry lifted his limp arm.

"The champion," he said.

"Murderer!" screamed Gertie.

"An accident," said Claude.

"Hammond didn't kill your sister," Gertie shouted, "I did!"

Very slowly Larry turned toward the Hammerheads. There were shots and poppies seemed to be growing all over Larry's robes. Then there were more shots.

By the time the cops arrived there was more dead meat on the floor than on the table. I quit. Let the cops work it out for themselves. And without a Hammerhead left to tell them what to think it would take them a long time. They were all dead, and I was glad. One of them had murdered Olivia, now it no longer mattered which. They were all guilty.

I had had a belly-full of Texas. Now I was in a hurry to go home. I took Hammond's car. I figured he owed me at least that. The hammer and sickle was swinging aimlessly in the wind as I passed through the gates for the last time. The ranch was ownerless, and there was no one left to inherit it. I turned on the car radio.

"Ladies and gentlemen," said a voice, "now it is midnight let us pause and give thanks that we live in the greatest country in the world. Our national anthem."

Tell it to the Indians. I drove on through the night. There was a lot of rain. In the morning there were rainbows. I kept my foot down. I was dreaming of Los Angeles where you get Hippo Hamburgers dressed with pickles and ice-cream all in one bun.

THE CREATURE ON
MY BACK

I have a creature on my back. It is invisible. No one knows it is there but me. It clings to my shoulders like an imp and tries to pull me to the ground. Paul Klee has written the line: "To stand despite all possibilities to fall." That about sums up my life. A constant struggle not to fall. In moments of despair I joke about the gravity of my situation. Naturally I can tell no one about the creature, what could I say? I envy hunchbacks, at least everyone can see the burden they carry.

I did not feel the creature climb on to my back. It was not there when I went to see the headhunter. I do not know why she is called a headhunter. She is not a hot-shot with a blow-pipe, a collector of shrunken heads, but just an agent who finds work for creative types in advertising agencies. She had landed me a two-week job writing the new campaign for Aphrodite — you know, the soap that put Aphro into Aphrodisiac. She was feeding chocolate drops to the Pekinese that was curled like a caddie above her crotch. Her scarlet lips smiled. She flattered me, but I too was insincere. Once when her dog was ill I telephoned to enquire after its health.

Aphrodite is manufactured by a multi-national giant. Player & Gamble. Player & Gamble is run like a holy order; equally concerned with converting the masses and preserving its own mysteries. Before I was allowed to work on their product I was compelled to take certain oaths. I was also handed a document entitled, "Player & Gamble Security Requirements". It contained a brief prolegomena on the necessity of security, followed by a series of commandments. 1. Thou shalt treat all documents from the originator as secret. 2. Thou shalt speak in a mutually understandable code when discussing P&G business over the telephone. 3. Thou shalt not talk of P&G in public places. Etcetera. Then there were the parables, telling of men led astray by "strangers", "reporters", "intruders", "men in dark glasses", "seductresses", and other agents of the Great Competitor. But I was not troubled. The new campaign became a great success.

However, the success did nothing for Sarah. Sarah is my wife. Poor Sarah was having a bad time. Late one night she came into my study.

"Well," she said, "it seems that I have been going through a very real emotional crisis."

I didn't take her seriously, which was a mistake.

"There is no such state as 'very real'," I said, "something is either real or it isn't."

"Jesus," she said.

"Further," I said, "to whom does 'it seem'? I bet you wouldn't have known a thing about it if good Dr Eggplant hadn't winkled out this 'emotional crisis'."

"His name is Dr Eckhardt," she said. She was grim-faced, white, breathing hard. None of them good signs.

"Well," I said, "it seems to me that these visits to Dr Eckhardt are doing you no good at all."

I had gone too far.

"JESUS CHRIST!" Sarah screamed. "I walk in and tell you I've practically had a nervous breakdown and all you do is give me literary criticism. All right, my use of language may not satisfy your precious New Critics, but I'm not talking about some book, I'm talking about me. I mean real life. I MEAN, DO I HAVE TO EXPRESS MY FEELINGS IN POETIC FORM BEFORE YOU'LL TAKE ANY NOTICE? Right! I'll tell you exactly what I'm feeling now, as precisely as possible. FUCK YOU!"

She slammed the door. The front door also slammed.

An hour later, when I was becoming frantic with worry, she returned. I apologised. We discussed Dr Eckhardt's findings seriously.

"Dr Eckhardt says," she said, "that my mind is stalling on a one-way track. It seems that this is messing up everything; it means that I am only functioning at one-third effectiveness."

Of course I knew what the real problem was. Sarah's shoulder was not wept upon. Too much of my life was hidden, even from

Sarah. This was my fault, but I could not correct it. We had talked it over many times, my self-sufficiency.

"So what remedy does the doctor recommend?" I asked.

"He doesn't know yet," she said. "He wants me to see him more often."

Without warning my heart swelled like a balloon. In truth, I was terrified of losing Sarah. Then the words came into my mind. I forced myself to voice them.

"Sarah," I said, "let's have a baby."

Sarah said she must ask Dr Eckhardt first.

He advised her to wait, explained that what she required was an egocentric not a concentric solution. He suggested that rather than have a baby she should experiment with infidelity. He said that it would do her more good than having a baby. Why? Because if she slept around she could choose her role, examine her options dispassionately, and control her emotions, letting them flow outward only when she decided. Thus growing emotionally self-sufficient.

"That's what you want, isn't it?" he said.

"I think so," said Sarah.

He told her that she must decide.

Sarah sat in his office, looking glum. She wasn't sure if she was ready to have a baby, but Dr Eckhardt's alternative was unattractive.

"I'll tell you what," said the doctor, "as a compromise try acting."

By coincidence they were planning the Christmas show at Sarah's school (Sarah being a teacher of history at Edgebrook High, a progressive establishment). After weeks of impassioned discussion, hours of self-analysis, careful examination of how the play would affect the teacher-kid relationship they threw out the classics and plumped instead for Picasso's *Four Girls*. They were thrilled with the inter-disciplinary nature of this, an opportunity to draw together the art and drama departments. The only serious objection came from some of the more conservative members of staff.

"Do you realise," they said, "that the characters are naked most of the play?"

This was hotly debated, but on a democratic vote the radicals prevailed. A motion by some militant women teachers that two of the girls should be played by boys was also carried.

"To force the kids to reevaluate their respective roles in society."

Casting did not take long. Sarah got her part by default. No one else wanted it.

"I have to slaughter a goat and drink its blood while I'm starkers," explained Sarah. "Dr Eckhardt is delighted."

Body-stockings were *de rigueur* during rehearsals. "To make sure you feel really naked on the night," said the director.

Unlike Dr Eckhardt I had misgivings. "Do you think this is the sort of thing the Head of History should be doing?" I asked. But I needn't have worried.

The press got hold of the story. WOMEN TEACHERS TO APPEAR NAKED WITH BOYS IN PICASSO SEX SHOW. There was a scandal. The production was killed.

"That's a relief," confessed Sarah.

She gets pregnant instead.

Lisa is the first person we tell. We are spending the evening with Lisa and Robin. Cross-legged on their floor watching television. Robin wrote the score for the Aphrodite commercial, a moody moog background to our lathered lady in the shower. So the pair of us sit; he a musician of some standing, having written for the Canadian National Ballet, but wanting to be a rock 'n roll star; me a novelist with sales below 1000, wanting to be as famous as Leonard Cohen; getting kudos from a soap commercial. Lisa accuses us both of exploiting women. She shakes her shapely head; her silver earrings shiver. A long man with an erect penis hangs from her left lobe, from her right dangles a woman with a swollen belly. Woman's fate. Lisa's fate.

Then Sarah announces, "I'm pregnant."

There is a knock at the door. Enter Helga and Ron. Helga is Robin's former wife, Ron is his best friend, best-man at their wedding. Ron is carrying a young boy, asleep in his arms; the son of Robin and Helga. He is put quietly into the bedroom which already contain's Eve and Mai; Lisa's daughters by Robin and her former husband. A couple of joints are lit up and passed around. Wine is poured. A wind blowing off Lake Ontario rattles the bamboo blinds and rustles the leaves of the avocado plants that stand on the window sills. We get very stoned.

"Do you know," says Lisa to Sarah, "when you said you were pregnant I didn't know whether to congratulate you or tell you the name of a good abortionist."

"Oh," says Sarah, "we definitely want it."

"Abortion is such an ugly word," says Helga, "though termination of pregnancy isn't any better."

"I know a terrible story about an abortionist," says Ron, "do you want to hear it?"

"Oh, yes!"

"Well, up in Catholic Quebec," begins Ron, "where a lot of people are still uptight about women — you know the French — abortions are not so readily available. I had this friend, a real nice lady, who got herself with child. The father didn't want to know about it. She can't turn to her family. Very upright. So she asks me for help. I find out the name of a woman who does douches, an old French woman who lives on a farm in the middle of nowhere. Batiscan, that's the place. We go there, one beautiful midwinter day. It doesn't take long. Walking away I notice drops of blood on the snow. Very dark blood. The miscariage was beginning. Twenty hours too early. Why am I telling you this? It's a horrible story. The girl died. Had a haemorrhage and bled to death. Shit! I wish I'd kept my mouth shut!"

Then the soap commercial reappears on the television. It makes us giggle. Even Ron who is crying and giggling at the same time.

Next morning something odd occurs while I am leafing through the newspaper. I become convinced that someone else is looking at it over my shoulder. I even know what article is being read. A report concerning the burial in Israel of two bars of soap. Made by the Nazis out of human fats. Sarah is being sick in the bathroom, I taste vomit in my mouth too, and feel a sudden spasm of pain between my shoulder blades, an embryonic kick in the back. What a grotesque spectacle that funeral must have been! What a metaphor for the human condition! I thank God I didn't know about this last night. Or I might have blurted it out like Ron's story of the dead girl. We would have invented a commercial for the soap. We would have giggled. In the bathroom I hear Sarah rinsing her mouth and washing her hands. If the Nazis had had their way she could be washing her hands with the mortal remains of Sigmund Freud.

When my pay from Player & Gamble arrives we decide to take a trip. To spend Easter in Quebec. We take the Turbo to Montreal. The woman in the seat behind starts to smoke a cigarette just as the train pulls out of the station. I turn around and tell her she's in a no-smoking section. The woman looks amazed. Without a word she gets up and walks away. Only the smoke remains, hovering like a ghost over her empty seat. We pick up speed as we skim through the townships of Oshawa and Nepanee. We flit through forests of pine and silver birch. Everywhere the snow is melting, so that the landscape looks like a half-finished painting. After Kingstown we follow the St Lawrence north-east on its course to Montreal.

Vieux Montréal is deserted in the icy drizzle of early Saturday morning. There are many antique shops full of objects from the back-country; especially expertly carved duck decoys. The fashion stores fill their windows with lady decoys. Sarah is finally attracted by one displaying a bright red dress. Inside the couturière has lifeless blonde hair and a lop-sided face. She is enormously tall. Sarah asks the price of the dress and when she exclaims it's way too much the lady drops the price by twenty dollars. Still too expensive, but Sarah decides to try it on. I watch her legs grow naked beneath the wooden door of the cubicle; and I am reminded of the shower scene in the soap commercial. Unexpectedly I feel a sudden fear of separation from Sarah.

I am beckoned. I see that Sarah has on a clinging dress made of some velvety material. Its main feature is the way it is cut in the front to show off the greater part of her tits. If she leaned forward you could see her nipples. The neckline is not a traditional V but open-ended so that the whole of her belly is also on show as though prepared for surgery. The woman is smiling horribly at me.

"It's a bit revealing, isn't it?" asks Sarah.

"There's a modesty flap you can sew on the front," says the lady, "most people do."

"I don't think so," says Sarah, "it's not for me."

"It fits you like a glove," says the woman. "I'll let you have it for thirty-five dollars."

I am no longer rational. I will be upset if Sarah buys the dress.

"No," she says.

"You are making a mistake," says the lady. She is annoyed.

"I don't know why she won't buy it," the woman says to me. "I made her a perfectly good offer."

I sense hostility between the shop-owner and myself, as though she blamed me for Sarah's refusal to buy.

"You didn't like that dress, did you?" says Sarah, when we are outside again.

"I hated it."

"I can't explain, but there was something creepy about that shop," says Sarah, "that woman, she reminded me of a witch from Grimm's fairy tales."

Or a wardress from a concentration camp.

We rent a car and drive out into the country for dinner. A note outside the restaurant reads: "After 6.00 pm we appreciate gentlemen wearing jackets and ties." That sort of place. We are seated beside a picture window. Beyond Lake Massawippi is frozen and floodlit, a seat of glass. It is a big dining-room, but there are no other diners. Loudspeakers hang from the wooden beams.

"What is the music?" I ask the waitress.

"Strauss waltzes," she says, "my favourite composer."

We order escargots to start; they come fat and juicy; they drip butter and taste of garlic. A man enters the dining-room; distinguished, wearing a jacket and tie; white-haired, ruddy-faced, blind drunk. He lurches across the room to the strains of "The Blue Danube", bumping into tables, attempting to stay on course with the aid of chair backs. The waitress sees him, rushes over, helps him to a seat. It is clear that the waitress is fond of him.

"Would you like something to eat, doctor?" she asks.

"I'm not hungry," he says, "just bring me a drink."

"Come on, Doc, you've got to eat something," the waitress says.

"Just bring me a drink!"

She goes to the bar.

"Terrible, terrible," mutters the doctor. "I've had a terrible day." He begins to moan.

We continue eating, but in the deserted dining-room the doctor is impossible to ignore. "Dr Eckhardt's ghost," jokes Sarah.

"Terrible, terrible," he repeats, again and again. Suddenly he pushes himself to his feet. His chair topples backwards but does not fall. "I don't want to live anymore!" he cries. He weaves a way around the wooden tables and walks sobbing out of the room. Before he vanishes I glimpse, fleetingly, the form of a homunculus clinging to his back.

We look like Lisa's earrings. Sara's naked, belly swelling. I'm erect. Our bodies have silver linings, outlined by light from the frozen lake. Sarah gasps as I enter her, feeling an expansion of flesh in flesh. Her breath comes in pants. HHH. HHH. Like a train. Our rhythms gather speed. Up and down. Like a train. My body concentrates, my thoughts freewheel. No smoking on this train. Verboten. You must have a shower. The doctor will give you a bar of soap. It's the woman from the dress shop. Aphrodite, the soap that put Aphro into Aphrodisiac. The doctor will turn you into a bar of soap. Herr Doktor. What if he is a Nazi doctor tormented by his past? GO AWAY!

"I'm coming! I'm coming!" screams Sarah.

She jerks, shudders to a halt. Then all thoughts are mercifully sucked from my mind. Swelling. Swelling. Swell . . . They say that the blood-soaked ground in Germany and Poland still cries out *in memoriam*. Here in Canada our only echoes from the past are visual, immediate, reflections. My favourite building in Toronto stands on the corner of York Street, a skyscraper that's like a giant mirror; looking as though a lake had been taken, poured into a rectangular receptacle, squared off, then placed in a vertical plane. Usually it is full of blue sky and puffs of cloud. Canada seems to have absorbed nothing; all thoughts, all feelings bounce off frozen surfaces and vanish in the unpolluted air.

On a back-country road heading north to Quebec. Driving through a peaceful valley. The dark pines on the hilltops give the sky a ragged edge. The air is luminous, the snow tinted rose-red by the sun, all dramatised by the fathomless cobalt sky. The bellies of the drifting clouds shine as their shadows cross the fields of snow. We are looking forward to our dinner in Quebec. Sarah says something, but I have no chance to reply. My head is suddenly jerked back, my fingers loosen their grip on the steering-wheel, and the car runs out of control. It swerves left across the road. I react instinctively; I pull the car back towards the right. For an instant I think I've got it under control. But the car hits black ice and I can't hold it.

"We're going!" I yell. I'm not thinking anymore. I put my arm around Sarah, shielding her. The other hand's still on the wheel but I can't do anything now. We shoot off the road at some crazy angle and for a second we're in the air. We tilt towards Sarah's side, but I've got her tight. Then there's a thump and we hit the ground and stop.

Dead silence.

"Sarah?" No reply. "SARAH?"

"I'm okay," she whispers. I put my hand on her belly. "That's all right, too," she says.

We blame the ice. The hook from the tow-truck bites into the car and heaves us back on to the road. No damage, not even a scratch. I do not tell Sarah that the creature on my back has tried to kill us. We dine in Quebec.

We breakfast at a café called Le Gaulois, among intellectual Quebecois. The man at the next table eats his fried egg in an ostentatious manner; he balances the unbroken yolk on his fork and takes it in one mouthful. Tiny yellow bubbles appear on his lips. We must hurry. The fast-flowing St Lawrence is filled with ice floes. It has been snowing all morning. Already there have been many accidents; cars colliding, unable to stop at crossroads. On the outskirts of Quebec I must make a decision: whether to stay north and go down to Montreal on Route 138, or to take the Trans-Canada Highway, south of the river.

"We'll start off on 138," I say, "but if the snow gets worse we'll cross to the Trans-Canada at Trois Rivières."

It gets much worse. The snow is no longer coming down in flakes, but rather in thin pencil lines, drawn horizontal by the wind, as though it were trying to fill in all the space around us with white. We are travelling in convoy now, a line of cars trying to follow the curve of the road (which, in turn, must be following the indentations of the river, lost in white) going slower and slower with each mile. We tick off the miles we do this way; the signposts

to Trois Rivières are regular; they appear every two miles: 30 to
go, 28, 26, 24. We're passing them every ten minutes or so. All
we have to do is keep this up.

But the weather isn't getting any better. "The blizzard, which
came in last night from the Great Lakes states has already dumped
a foot of snow on Montreal, and as yet shows no sign of abating,"
says the man on the car radio. So we've been driving into the blizzard all day! "Watch out for 'white-outs'," warns the man. What?
On an exposed flank of a curve in the road, with the wind blowing
directly at us from across the river a "white-out" is defined; the
car is suddenly immersed in snow, swept over by a wave of white
nothingness which hits the windshield with a splat. At about four
in the afternoon we pass the 22-mile marker. The weather continues to worsen; even without "white-outs" the visibility is practically nil. Sarah is very tense. We cross the Petite Rivière Batiscan.
There are huge drifts on either side of the road. Snow is blowing
wildly off the tops. Not only must I keep the car going down this
narrow alley between the banks of snow, avoiding abandoned
trucks, without thinking about oncoming traffic, but now I've got
to do it blindfold. It is as if the creature on my back has expanded
to fill the whole world, and it is this shrieking banshee of a world
that I am fighting as I wrestle with the steering-wheel. Finally,
blinded, I drive straight into a drift. We're stuck.

"What shall we do?" says Sarah.

I haven't a clue.

Between gusts of wind I can make out a house about one hundred yards to our right, and I think I can see someone moving
about in there. We remain where we are until it begins to get dark,
expecting rescue; but no one comes, nor any snow ploughs. The car
is almost buried; we must leave. We can just open my door wide
enough for us to squeeze out. We have decided to make for the
house. Beyond the door is bedlam. The wind is so loud we cannot
speak; it rushes at us like an animal, clawing us with snow. Given
the chance it would rip our clothes and our bodies too. We clamber
to the top of the drift so that we are on a level with the car roof,
and we begin to walk in the direction of the house. We see it as a
flickering light. In seconds we're soaked. Already we're panting.
Snow is hurled non-stop against us, icy air flies up our nostrils. It

is difficult to brea..ne.

The light has almost gone from the day. More, the known world has been obliterated as utterly as at Pompeii. Through the gloom we can see the house glimmering, the only certain fixture in the landscape. I hold Sarah tight. Twice the creature tries to take her from me as she is sucked into the soft snow; twice I pull her back. The snow is deepest here, the high drifts around the house, but now we're past them too, slipping down towards the back door of the place. Sanctuary.

We can smell wood smoke, a wonderful smell.

An old man opens the door. Dressed in a faded blue French peasant smock. He fusses around us, concerned to see that we don't drip on the linoleum. A fat woman (about the right age to be his daughter) takes our coats and hats and hangs them near the stove. She has a few words of English.

"Welcome," she says. "Please sit down with the others." She beckons us through the cheerful kitchen with its great wood-burning stove into the L-shaped living-room.

The ancient has already returned, sitting in his rocking-chair, listening to the radio. We are introduced to the woman's husband, a Gallic type; his shoulders poised permanently on the point of a shrug. At the table half-a-dozen other refugees from the storm sit drinking gin. I tick off the characters: the smooth travelling sales-man, the joker with the goatee beard, his silent resentful wife, a pretty girl with a diamond engagement ring, an unrelated moody youth who clenches his fists in response to some inner tension, the old lady with the lap dog. Eight strangers trapped by the raging blizzard. A favourite movie plot.

Actually there is an old movie on the television in the other part of the room which no one is watching, a Randolph Scott yarn dubbed into French. Above the set, pinned to the wall, is Christ crucified. A bookcase is filled with religious texts, mainly on Catholicism. At the end of the L stands a piano upon which rests a coloured photograph of a young girl in nurse's uniform; I assume it is of the woman's daughter, but upon closer inspection it seems altogether too old-fashioned. We find the bathroom, a doorless cubicle in the couple's bedroom, containing both toilet and sink. The bedroom is gloomy; there is another cross on the wall and plastic flowers in vases on the dressing-table, alongside many pills for the symptoms of old age. Conversation continues at the table. Only the boy has departed, gone around the corner to watch the cowboy film.

"We did not expect the snow," says the farmer in French, "we were planning to tap our maple trees today. But now the sap has frozen again."

I wander back to the television. The commercials are on; would you believe it, it's Aphrodite again! The kid seems to fancy the girl in the shower. I do not like the look of him, those clenched fists; I fear that later, in the night, he will try to rape Sarah.

We sleep fully-clothed on the sofa. We are not disturbed. But at dawn Sarah rises and rushes to the cubicle in the bedroom where she is sick several times. Later the farmer's wife looks carefully into her pale face and says,

"Are you sure you came here by accident, my dear, you weren't looking for me, were you?" She stares at me and says, "Are you the father?"

I am speechless. Where are we? Then I remember. BATISCAN. Is it possible? Have we landed up with the abortionist who killed Ron's friend? I calm down, no need to be over-dramatic. This woman is not evil; most probably she thinks she is doing us a kindness, thinks we need coaxing before we'll admit why we have come. But how can she be an abortionist? She is Catholic.

"It is very clean here," says the woman, opening the bedroom door for our inspection, showing us the cubicle with its spotless sink and the two bars of soap. "There is no danger, I used to be a nurse."

I am helpless, the creature on my back has its hands firmly clasped over my mouth.

"Come into the cubicle, my dear," she says to Sarah, "and let me examine you."

I cry out, "Don't go!" but the words are soundless. I cannot help Sarah.

"You're mistaken," says Sarah, "I want the baby."

As Sarah's belly grows so do my struggles with the creature on my back. I wrestle with it constantly. In the mornings it attempts to hold me to the bed. During the day it tries to throw me to the ground. Even at nights I am not free. I dream that I am pinned to the floor and must watch helpless while a bloody embryo is torn from Sarah's open belly. The thing is made of soap. At last I confide in Sarah. But the confession does not lift the weight from my shoulders. So Sarah suggests that I see her shrink. Next I tell Dr Eckhardt about the creature on my back. He walks around me.

"I can see nothing," he says.

"It is there, none the less," I say.

"Well, you are a *mensh*, you know life is a struggle," says Dr Eckhardt, "there is a Yiddish saying: 'Shoulders are from God, and burdens too'."

"Why my shoulders?" I ask.

"Listen," says Dr Eckhardt, "you are lucky. You have a creature on your back. Such things are not common in Canada. It may yet go away. As for myself, I have a number on my arm. A souvenir of Europe."

AMONG SCHOOL CHILDREN

Since our flat lacks a phone I have to do the inviting from the booth near Wardour Street. As I wait to make the calls a girl approaches me and says, "Piss off, mister, this is my patch." Inside the booth I spread out the two-penny pieces on the spines of the directories and I begin.

"Hello," I say, "Sophie and I are getting married next Wednesday. There's a party afterwards at our place. Can you come?" I notice as I talk that the windows are covered with obscene graffiti, so that Soho is overlaid with CUNTS scribbled crudely, and the dialling codes are obscured by the calling cards of prostitutes, one of whom is also named Sophie. I consider phoning this vulgar variant, but I would not desert Sophie for such an ape of love. I get plenty of opportunities in my job, and take none of them.

I am a photographer by trade, and even now I am shocked by what girls will do in front of my camera, those faceless girls who touch themselves on my say-so. More than once as I focus down on the pressed curls of pubic hair that cling to the brownish folds of flesh held apart for my benefit I am reminded of a reptilian eye, and the musky smell that fills my nostrils and my mouth seems entirely appropriate.

Our wedding goes off without a hitch, but the party turns out to be a disaster. Someone asks me if Sophie has any faults.

"Only one," I say, "she will leave the bath full of her pubic hair. And when she shaves her legs. . . ."

Hearing that Sophie blows up. "You fastidious little worm!" she cries. And so we have the first row of our married life. However, that is but the prelude to the real disaster.

Around midnight our clapped out lavatory backfires. And a guest emerges, somewhat flushed, pursued by a torrent of water-borne shit. My closest friends stay to help with the cleaning up.

everyone else goes home. Sophie locks herself in the bedroom.

"Best to take things like this philosophically," I am advised. Exactly. Plato thought this world but a shadow of some better substance, but that is only half the truth. For this world of ours rests on a bed of shit. And every so often it breaks through.

Sophie continues to refuse to speak to me. So I retire to my darkroom. I am no artist, no creator, merely limited by my camera to mimesis, to producing shadows of shadows; even so I still feel a thrill when the image first appears on the Kodak paper suspended in the developer. Somehow the finished prints never quite live up to this promise. Thus I spend my wedding night; reviving images of naked girls; first grains, then ghosts, then full-bodied women, a host of succubae.

Nevertheless, the first year of our marriage is happy. We even dine in civilised fashion with my parents. Indeed, every time we visit their house my mother insists upon giving Sophie a dress or a skirt or a jumper that she claims no longer fits. By our second anniversary Sophie seems to be dressing exclusively in my mother's clothes. One night, as we embrace and I begin to unbutton Sophie's blouse, it occurs to me that, in close-up, the floral-pattern blouse could as well be on my mother to whom it once belonged. Immediately my erection goes spineless. From that moment fucking Sophie becomes a problem; in fact I can only function at all if the conditions are exactly right. To convince me that she is not my mother Sophie has to act the whore; I demand utter wantonness. Sophie, fortunately, is very patient; the result of years as a teacher. Which reminds me of one of my more curious assignments; shooting the illustrations for a limited edition of the Yeats poem, "Among School Children". On the quiet, without parental permission, young girls are brought to my studio and photographed in the nude; dreadful creatures who make dirty jokes about the Vaseline I rub on my lens and pout like they're posing for David Hamilton. "Jailbait", my assistant calls them, and lays them one after another. What they need is a good wallop or a harsh reproof. "Solider Aristotle played the taws," says Yeats, "upon the bottom of a king of kings." So Sophie kneels naked before our bed, at my insistence, arms outstretched legs splayed so that her bottom is open and defenseless. As I hit her with lochgelly taws I chant from "Among School Children" until I gob helplessly over her bent back at the lines, "Plato thought nature but a spume that plays upon a ghostly paradigm of things."

Come to think of it, there is another habit of Sophie's that drives me mad, which must come from all the teaching she does; we have some friends who have two daughters, whom Sophie will never call by name but always "girls". One of them is called Cathy.

It is high summer, the third summer of our marriage. We are in the northern town of Y—, looking after Cathy and her sister while the parents holiday in Venice. The sunshine is brilliant, Devochka, white-walled and Georgian, stands illuminated amid lawns of shimmering green; Cathy and sister, both in white, romp with Podger, off-spring of an Old English Sheepdog and an unknown tramp who led the silly bitch up the garden path. The scent of flowers hangs heavy, bees fill the foxgloves. Sophie and I sit on wicker chairs, sipping gin-and-tonics, watching the girls play. Cathy's hair is dark and short, strands clinging to her damp forehead, her eyes are brown and wide. She is ten years and eleven months; of an age but a world apart from the girls in my studio; not a little but a "liddell" girl. When she smiles her lips reveal her secret; they bud like those of Alice Liddell, photographed ages ago by the perspiring Reverend Charles Lutwidge Dodgson. As Cathy flickers across the lawn she continually brings to mind fading images from old albums; Dymphna Ellis, dreamy Amy Hughes and the incredible Irene Macdonald who (at the age of eight or nine) has the eyes and mouth of an Eastern courtesan, all of whom wrung groans from poor tormented Dodgson. Then the summer light grows umbral, and Cathy's bare arms and legs glow sepia from woody reflections. Evocative new images develop; for example, Rejlander's astonishing photographs of little girls in the most provocative poses, bare tantalising things, artfully lit to give a heart-rending illusion of vitality. Of course such things are not real. However, sometimes, looking at Cathy, the image and the reality appear to coincide; her knife-edge innocence seems immortal, tangible; she exists without implication of a future life. She is the promise that all women break when they assume roles as lovers, virgins, wives and mothers; she is the blueprint which her growth will betray. But her present quality cannot be possessed;

that is the paradox that frustrates, for any act of possession will be the act of destruction. To follow the desires that Cathy excites will render her immaculate no longer, for she will be made self-conscious. My passion for Cathy must remain Platonic. Instead I shadow her through the garden, round the house, with my loaded camera; trying to capture her spirit.

Each morning I wake full of hope and lie supine staring at the ceiling to watch the chandelier fill with rainbows as the sun rises. Sophie sleeps on for an hour or so longer and sometimes I examine her face and those parts of her body exposed by the eiderdown. My love for Sophie has changed, I no longer want to possess her; recently our love-making has become an elaborate disguise for masturbation. Actually we have not touched one another since our arrival at Devochka, and I feel much refreshed. After getting up we take turns to visit the water closet, a special feature of this remarkable house; it consists of a bowl of white porcelain decorated with blue laurels, encased in a frame and seat of ruddy mahogany; soon such visits are known as "resting on your laurels". At breakfast as usual Cathy says, "What shall we do today?"

Today we plan to take the girls to Haworth. In our different ways both Sophie and I have connections with Emily Bronte, erstwhile inhabitant of Haworth Parsonage; Sophie, because she teaches *Wuthering Heights* for the English Literature "A" Level; myself, because I once had to shoot a lurid photograph of a dark man whipping a naked girl for a paperback edition billed as "the strangest love story ever told". Cathy and her sister loll in the back of the car with Podger between them, giggling at some secret joke, while Sophie sits beside me with the map. The way through the northern moorland is desolate and exciting, mist floats over the greyish-green ground and above the patches of purple heather that look like bruises, such a change from the dazzling clarity of the preceeding days. Shadows solidify into boulders; shapes become grazing ponies. Sophie and Cathy's sister play at guessing what other shapes will become, but Cathy sits silently and her eyes stay fixed gazing out over the wilderness.

The Parsonage stands at the end of a steep and cobbled main street. Halfway up this street is a sweet-shop, which boasts of its home-made produce. The owner, a fat man with a black mous-

tache and greasy hair, wears a transparent plastic glove to dip his
sinister hand into the fruit fudge and the rum truffles, the same
perfumed hand with which, to my disgust, he pats the cheek of
Cathy, who smiles like a little flirt. Most of the visitors to the
Parsonage seem to be old ladies satisfied to see a slipper "said to
have fitted Emily Bronte's foot", unconscious of the tragic para-
doxes with which she struggled, not hearing an echo of Heathcliff's
dreadful cry, "I could almost see her, and yet I could not!" Poor
Heathcliff, tortured by the eternal absence of Catherine, who yet
remained close enough to haunt him. Standing alone, dreaming in
the play-room with its quietened toys and pencil drawings on the
cream walls, Cathy's sudden appearance makes me jump.

"Those toys look fun," says Cathy, "whose were they?"

"Emily Bronte's," I say. "Have you heard of her?"

"Oh, yes," says Cathy, "she wrote *Wuthering Heights*."

"Have you read it?" I ask.

"Oh, no," says Cathy, "it's much too grown-up for me."

In Plato's *Symposium* Aristophanes proposes that love is "the
desire and pursuit of the whole". Hence Heathcliff's mania to be
reunited, literally, with his Catherine. Hence also my obsession
with Cathy. I am convinced that I can be made whole by Cathy,
but I have no idea how to go about this reunification.

We eat by candlelight in the middle of the huge dining-room,
our intimacy emphasised by the space and the gathering darkness
beyond our illuminated circle. We all drink white wine which
sparkles in tall crystal glasses. Cathy insists upon finishing off a
whole glass.

And so we sit until Sophie says, "Come on, girls, you must be
dog-tired, it's time for bed."

Podger yawns under the table. Cathy rises, claims to be drunk,
giggles and falls flat on her back; whereupon her frock of corn-
flowers, purchased at a jumble sale, obeys its own gravity and falls
up her legs, showing off her creamy panties which are caught
tight between the cheeks of her bum. Her older sister blushes.
Later Sophie returns and says,

"They want you to say goodnight to them." So I visit their
bedroom and kiss Cathy and her sister and Cathy's teddy-bear. In
the lounge Sophie is already reclining on the settee, right hand

limp among the tassels, so I take my place in the armchair opposite, and we begin to talk. I don't know if it is because of the wine but gradually my mind withdraws from the conversation and soon Sophie is talking to herself. I watch her alter and realter her position, as if she were a model posing for one of my photographic sessions; first she rests her arm above her head, her hand in her hair, revealing that smooth, sweeping concavity between the soft uppers of her arm and the bare skin of her side; then she bends toward me so that her jumper falls free of her body and her breasts are exposed. She is saying something which I do not catch. Suddenly Sophie jumps up.

"I saw the way you looked at Cathy's crotch," she says. I deny it. "Wouldn't you prefer mine?" she says, pulling down her skirt and pants. "Look," she says, pointing a moist finger at my face, "it wants you."

"What are you, a tart?" I shout.

"No, I'm your wife," cries Sophie, "and I want you to fuck me!"

"I'm taking Podger for a walk," I say. I breathe in the night air. I know that Sophie is trapped in a role of my making, one which I now realise fills me with disgust.

Next morning Cathy says, "Why is Sophie in such a bad mood?"

"I'm not," says Sophie. And she insists upon preparing breakfast for us all.

I can tell by the way her shoulder blades pull together as she slices the bread that she is fighting her anger and the humiliating knowledge that she is jealous of Cathy. Once again the sun blazes in a vacant blue sky as we tour the abbey ruins of Rievaulx and Fountains, trying to recreate the original vision from the standing foundations, for these foundations have become our blue-prints. At Fountains Abbey Cathy sinks into the river up to the hem of her dress which subsequently clings to her knees as she runs up and down the wooded inclines. The sun is setting now and beams of light pour through the gaping holes in the ruined walls, like a projector ray through film, so that I am tempted to search the eastern sky for images from the Abbey's past, as if we were at a drive-in movie. The light also shines through Cathy's dress, outlining her body, filling me with such a longing I almost groan. But a longing for what? Aristophanes adds in the *Symposium*, "It is clear that the soul of each (lover) has some other longing which it cannot express, but can only surmise and obscurely hint at." A fat lot of good that does me, my craving is such that if I get no relief I fear what might happen.

"Look what I can do!" yells Cathy, pointing to a stone that goes skimming over the surface of the water, as flighty as her affection for me.

The ruins of Bolton Abbey are on a long sweep of parkland, which unrolls down toward a broad river, at which black and white cows with lengthening shadows are drinking. I wander off to explore the remains by myself, and feel slightly uneasy to be alone in that spiritual place at twilight. Much of the chapel is still intact, and as I approach the impressive portico, quietly over the stone pavement, I am startled to hear the sound of an organ rising from the darkness within; the notes, made of wind and air, are discordant and melancholy. Inside I can just make out a small boy fiddling at the keyboard, and as I stare into the gloom I feel a small cold hand slip into mine.

"I don't like to be alone in the dark," whispers Cathy, "can I hold your hand?" Her fingers tickle my palm.

Outside the first stars are shining. Cathy's sister wants to know if it is true that some of the stars we can see are no longer there.

"Yes, dear," says Sophie, "because they are so far away their light takes a long time to reach us, longer than their lives." To be nothing more than light, like Alice Liddell and those other Victorian girls, images left behind of a single moment of perfection.

I am dreading the night, sure that once more Sophie will try to force me into love-making. I do not see how I can face it, tormented as I am by Cathy. But I am wrong, Sophie simply announces that when we return to London she is going to leave me. She switches out the light. But I cannot sleep. Hours later I am roused from an unsatisfactory doze by the sound of Podger barking. I go downstairs and find the dog shivering from a nightmare. I stroke him till he relaxes once more. Then I listen to the silence of the sleeping house and I am filled with disquiet. Returning upstairs I notice that the bathroom light is on; inside stands Cathy, oblivious of my presence. Now I have seen all manner of naked women, but none of them has ever moved me as I am by the sight of Cathy standing there, slowly lifting her flannel nightgown over her head. Her body shines in the neon light; two Cathies; herself and her image in the looking-glass. The first begins to examine the second, and I do likewise and see in her body the embryo of all my desires; around her breasts there is a barely perceptible swelling, a slight pinkish flush, and below her belly are her labial palps, still uncovered, oh my palpitating heart. And watching I weep, because I know that I will never be able to fix that image in the mirror.

My desires at last take concrete form, I have an erection that cannot be denied. Of course I consider approaching Cathy, but apart from anything else I am not certain how to go about such things with a pre-pubescent girl. So I return reluctantly to the bedroom. Once behind the closed door I pull the quilt off Sophie and ponder her naked body.

At length I wake her and say, "Sophie, if you shave off all your pubic hair I'll fuck you."

"Piss off, mister," she says, "I'm not removing my patch for you." So I hit her until she is too weak to put up any resistance; then I straddle her and with a pair of nail scissors snip off her pubic hair to the roots. The stubble looks so unsightly that Sophie agrees to remove it with the Veeto cream that she now uses on her legs. She rubs it over the grey triangle, between her legs and even in her anus.

"So you've turned out to be a poofter like Ruskin," says Sophie.

"I can't explain," I say, "just do it, please."

"It burns like hell," says Sophie.

"I'm sorry," I say. But eventually the inflammation subsides and Sophie's belly is completely smooth.

"Let me look at you," I say.

Sophie, also curious, examines herself in the mirror. For a second I see in her reflection the image of Cathy. "And thereupon my heart is driven wild: she stands before me as a living child."

TITILLATIO

Bedded in her double-divan wedded Bella, miles away, is suddenly robbed of her senses and instinctively buttock-shoves husband Quentin deeper inside of her, responding at last to his pumping with helpless spasms of her own until, with a final cry of "I'm coming!" she reaches her climax.

"How do you feel?" asks Quentin.

"Good," says Bella, yawning, and promptly falling asleep. Quentin, too, after wiping himself with a Kleenex, nods off.

Bella, next morning, hears the phone ring. She picks up the receiver.

"What are you doing?" the other end asks.

"I am writing about ethics," she replies.

"I don't know much about ethics," the man says, "but I know what I like." This remark is somewhat ingenuous, since the speaker (a famous Professor of Philosophy) is in fact the supervisor of Bella's thesis.

"And what do you like?" whispers Bella, assuming a familiar role.

"Bathing you," he answers, "feeling your soap-smooth skin, smelling a mixture of you and the talc."

Bella smiles. He isn't like that, really. And knowing him well, as she does, she recognises that he is excited and that he is, however obscure the origin of his impulse, attempting to involve her in the same experience. She knows exactly what he wants.

"Tonight," she whispers.

"Tonight," he agrees.

Do not be misled into thinking that Bella is whispering for the sake of any extraneous erotic effect, on the contrary it is a necessary precaution, because her eldest daughter (aged twelve) is now standing in the doorway behind her, requiring maternal attention.

The husband, as is often the case, knows nothing about the true nature of his wife's relationship with her academic mentor. There is, moreover, an especial irony in his situation; for it was he who finally persuaded Bella to take her Masters degree, and who felt the greatest pride in her achievement when she was invited to complete her doctorate. Such is the bad luck of a husband who encourages his wife to be, simultaneously, a Master of Arts and the mistress of an ageing Professor of Philosophy. But if we say that Quentin is a builder of bridges we are not making fun of the cuckold, we are talking about his occupation. Quentin's achievements at linking opposite banks of a river filled his doting, spoiling mother with a perverse joy; for had her own husband (Quentin's father) not died beside the River Kwai? This suggestion of son-succeeding-where-father-failed gives Quentin a sense of security (expressed outwardly in the ancient sturdy home that houses his family), and in reflective moments he is wont to view his happy predicament with genial satisfaction. Nor does the smile leave his fond face when his younger daughter (aged eleven) comes in with the news that he has to prepare dinner tonight because Mummy has to go to an important meeting at the university.

Needless to say, the important meeting (if that is what we choose to call it) does not take place at the university, but rather in a flat rented by the prophetic Professor of Philosophy for just such occasions. The apartment is bare; a single large room containing nothing but a double-bed. A key is inserted into a lock, a door opens, our illicit couple enters. Perhaps we may pause to wonder just what there is about this fifty-five-year-old professor that has so captivated his thirty-year-old student. Hair: grey, thick at sides, thin on top. Eyes: also grey, surrounded by laughter lines, underlined by bags.

"Just as a hotel receptionist is suspicious of a guest who arrives without luggage," says the Professor, "so you should be wary of a man without bags. He will not stay with you longer than a night." His mouth, then, is witty and wise. His voice is generally gentle, though it can be stern, whereupon it reveals a continental accent. He has a nose to match; large, slightly curved. His chief vanity is his assumed resemblance to Saul Bellow. We could go on, but will it make Bella's infatuation any easier to understand? Indeed, the whole affair will appear even more improbable when we reveal that, for the past few years, the Professor of Philosophy has been, more or less, impotent.

They have never made love properly. This is what generally happens: Bella undresses and lies supine on the bed, while the Professor touches, strokes her compliant responsive flesh, slowly but clearly exciting her, until she directs his hand herself, moving her pelvis up and down, rubbing herself against his firm fingertip, stimulating her clitoris, ticklish at first, then tenser, till her orgasm comes. While Bella concentrates all of herself to this one end the Professor is, as it were, left alone with his thoughts. He remembers, with a certain degree of embarrassment, Spinoza's "active emotions" of which joy or *hilaritas* is the chief and most vital expression of the whole personality, whereas sensuous pleasure or *titillatio* is but the automatic reaction to the local stimulation of an organ. Sometimes Bella's transports convince him that she is indeed expressing a joy that comes from her whole being, and then allows her to deal in a like manner with his own out-of-tune organ so that, by dint of prolonged fondling, and perhaps some further oral persuasion, he too has an orgasm.

Tonight, in the flat, the Professor introduces a variation. As he makes his way, in his familiar meticulous fashion, over Bella's naked body, he gives her a running commentary.

"Here's Bella's flat belly, and down this slope, down here, between her thighs, there's a slit, covered with curly hair; you can open it up, and inside are damp, shiny folds of pinkish flesh, and now there's her smell and this little knob — shall I go on?"

"Please."

"What will happen if I touch just here?"

"Yes, yes, yes, touch." Bella closes her eyes and awaits the moving finger.

Afterwards, laughing with pleasure and relief, she curls up on the bed, cuddles up against her man, and begins to hum an old song, "My Heart Belongs to Daddy".

Bella's own father was the head-waiter in a large hotel on the South Coast of England in the austere but tranquil post-war years. Her late mother, unfortunately, had artistic aspirations, which led her to desert her husband for the fading intellectual blossoms of

Bloomsbury, leaving everything behind, including her daughter. But poor little Bella was not destined to spend happy hours with Papa either; after just a few months alone together he packed Bella off to London, packed his own belongings and vanished forever, leaving his daughter with half-remembered memories of seaside walks and talks on sandy windswept beaches. Very different to serving tea to homosexual authors, wine to artists who sported velvet hats and fucked heiresses for their livelihood, and cigarettes to poets who dedicated their lives to finding a rhyme for Eliot. Quentin's mother appeared at one such soiree, as these gatherings were known, and in time Bella and Quentin were introduced. Quentin was handsome and Bella was young, well-developed, eager to learn the mysterious ways of a man with a maid. She got pregnant at the age of seventeen, and married soon after; but that is just as they wanted it because, have no doubts, they were in love. From the very beginning Quentin was anxious that his new wife should be happy, so he initiated his dangerous policy of allowing her to make most decisions for them both. From a mere indulgence this grew into a way of life that characterised their whole relationship, until Bella became the dominant partner in the marriage, and more and more impatient with Quentin's inability to make up his mind on any subject without first consulting her.

Such is the explanation (for which Quentin searched in vain) of Bella's otherwise inexplicable behaviour on the night of their thirteenth wedding anniversary.

Quentin suggested that they dine out. Bella agreed, a baby sitter was obtained to look after the girls. There remained only the decision about the restaurant. Although Bella kept maintaining that she couldn't care less where they ate, she took considerable trouble over her appearance, and finally emerged from the bathroom with false eyelashes, lashings of mascara, rosy cheeks and brand-new lipstick; dressed also in the long gown reserved exclusively for special events. But Quentin had no table booked, and by the time he had decided where to try it was too late to get a table anywhere; so they ended up on their thirteenth anniversary dining in the local pizza parlour. It was there, when Quentin was dallying over the wine list, that Bella had hysterics. Quentin was amazed, he couldn't understand why Bella was so upset. It never occurred to him that sometimes Bella simply wanted to have a fuss made of her, wanted to be taken out for treats; in effect, she wanted all the delights due to a favourite daughter. But this role Bella fancied for herself was constantly undermined by the presence of her own children; frequently she wondered where these two human beings could have come from, it seemed inconceivable that they could have emerged from her womb. When they were born she had refused to breast-feed either one. She was frightened by their dependence upon her; later she came to feel that the whole security of their home was founded upon a lie, for she was too weak to carry the burden of all their lives; secretly Bella longed to be dependent upon someone else. She chose the Professor of Philosophy.

Therefore, one night (soon after that disastrous thirteenth wedding anniversary) the Professor was astonished to have his flirtatious banter returned with a passion that, in a single moment, threw into question thirty-five years of self-doubt. The Professor was even more astonished when he later learned that Quentin was a most competent lover (unlike himself). But it was Quentin's very competence that worked against him; for in his love-making with Bella he neither asked for anything, nor ever needed help, so that the whole became a process of giving, for the benefit of Bella; on the other hand, with the Professor, it was Bella who gave the pleasure, Bella who sometimes made him come. You will observe, then, how unfair are the ways of the heart; for when Bella wanted to be dominated Quentin was passive, but when Quentin was active, under the sheets, between her thighs, was the very time that Bella required a sign of weakness. This is what Bella wanted: she wanted a man who was strong in the eyes of the world, but whose very strength concealed secret fallibilities, which she alone knew, which she alone could overcome.

After a final chorus of "My Heart Belongs to Daddy" Bella looks up into the face of the Professor and, seeing acquiescence there, begins to kiss his balls and lick his penis, until she can feel upward jerks and the thing beginning to grow beneath her mouth. The Professor gazes with gratitude at this girl who will do anything for him, but he is still wise enough to know that self-gratification is, by itself, a form of bondage.

"When I am driven to an act by external stimuli or by desire, such as I now have, I am not truly free," he reasons, "for neither Bella's action nor my desire is rational, and so long as it remains irrational I am a slave to my passions."

By this time his penis is very big.

"We say that we love one another, yet if love ceases to be an agent of goodness it is surely a false love, and our love threatens the happiness of five other people; no, I am certainly not free," concludes the Professor. Simultaneously his penis stabs the air and his glans opens releasing little spurts of semen.

"Was it good?" asks Bella.

"I think so," answers the Professor.

Bella laughs and wipes her mouth with a Kleenex.

"Why am I doing this?" wonders the Professor. "Why am I allowing it to happen to me?"

Once, when the Professor had actually voiced these doubts to Bella she had said, "Fuck Spinoza. Listen to Kant."

The Professor had listened.

"Freedom is the choice you make in deciding whether or not you submit to your passion or submit to your duty," Bella had said, "so make up your mind, mister, passion or duty?"

But even as the Professor surrendered to his instincts he tried to discern if his affair with Bella was the result of a unique coincidence of personalities or merely a coincidence of events. Destiny or opportunity? However, none of these worries prevented him from continuing. Despite his wisdom he had no answer to his student's tongue.

"Titillatio."

"Fellatio."

"Spinoza."

"Spermatozoa."

"Kant."

"Cunt." She got him every time. Thus unadulterated pleasure can make a hypocrite and an adulterer of the most ethical of men.

Quentin, as we have noted, considers that he is happy, blessed with a trouble-free life; which just goes to show that men who are accustomed to scrutinising every detail to ensure that the bridges they build will not topple are not necessarily the best judges when it comes to an assessment of the grounds upon which they base their own existence. He assumes, in his complacency, that he has constructed a secure family unit for himself, supported by foundations that are sunk deep into the love that he and Bella share. And he could have been right, had he not forgotten the simple fact that marriage is a dynamic state, and that fundamentals which were true ten years ago need no longer be in operation a decade later. Both he and Bella have developed as personalities in the time they have lived together, but their relationship has not grown, indeed it has become repressed, smothered by Quentin's feather-brained pillow of easy acquiescence.

We've already made a flippant reference to the beginnings of Quentin's career as a builder of bridges so, in fairness, we should add a few more details. For the truth of the matter is that Quentin had wanted to be an engineer from the moment he received his first Meccano set; and all the troubled years between puberty and manhood were spanned by balsa-wood replicas of the world's greatest bridges. Indeed, so good were some of the models that Quentin still displays them in his private study. He is relaxing in a leather armchair in that very room when Bella returns (so he thinks) from her university meeting.

"Hello," she says, "are the children in bed?"

"Hours ago," replies Quentin, without a trace of sarcasm; although Bella is back late it does not occur to him to be annoyed.

"Did you have a good meeting?" he asks.

"I enjoyed myself," Bella replies, truthfully.

Although, as we've disclosed, the Professor (*pace* conscience) is content in the progress of his affair with Bella, it would be a mistake to assume that he will be satisfied to let things continue the way they are. He feels, in some odd way, that it would be somehow selfish of him, egocentric, as it were, and that he ought to give pleasure as well as receive it. He is a man after all, and he considers that fifty-five is too early an age to bid farewell to his potency forever. However, as he does not understand the cause of his own impotence, indeed had been amazed to discover that he was impotent, he is quite powerless to reassert his previous prowess. Is it, he asks himself, some ill-defined punishment on his wife's behalf for all those times he had made loveless love to her, regular as clockwork, with his cock hooded like some thief in the night? Having decided that one unknowable daughter was sufficient. Is it something to do with Kant? If Bella's analysis was correct, and freedom is the choice between passion and duty, and if he had clearly decided to go along with passion, why then was his penis not acting in accordance with his will? Does it mean that he is not a free man after all, that he is, in effect, the captive of a duty he does not comprehend? Is Kant's unanswerable criterion that one should act "as if the maxim of your actions were to become by your will law universal" putting a block on his animal instincts? The Professor of Philosophy, a rational man, is perplexed. It does not occur to him that there is something darker, less flattering, in his passion; and at the root of his impotence. So we leave him, still in two minds, once more dialling the number of his mistress.

"According to Kinsey," says Bella to Quentin as the telephone starts to ring, "some psychoanalysts contend that they have never had a patient who has not had incestuous relationships. Sort of kith and Kinsey. Don't worry, I'll get it."

"What is the significance of that?" asks Quentin. But Bella is already whispering into the receiver.

"Bet you didn't know," says Bella, returning to the conversation, "that if unofficial American estimates are anything to go by seventy-eight per cent of all incestuous relationships are between father and daughter, while only one per cent occur between mother and son. So I'll be keeping an eye on you, Daddy."

"Don't be daft," says Quentin.

Over the telephone the Professor of Philosophy had invited Bella to the farewell party of one of his more eccentric graduate students; an American, shortly to be deported for possession of a small amount of cocaine. Bella, who rather liked the American, accepted at once, and now informs her husband that she will have to go out two nights hence.

The party begins quietly, and though that soon changes it does not have much effect upon the Professor and Bella who stand chatting over chalices of Spanish Burgundy, that is, until the curly American asks Bella to dance. Actually, Bella's American host was rather glad to see her arrive, gladder still to see her without her husband. Innocent, he assumes that an estrangement has occurred, and that Bella has come round to him for comfort. Needless to say, he is quite ignorant of her affair with the Professor, as his actions will testify; however anarchic, all American graduates have a highly developed sense of academic hierarchy. The music's rocking, Rolling Stones stuff, but still he holds her tight. The Professor, who has never before had any reason to doubt Bella's devotion, is suddenly seized by jealousy, a juvenile luxury, and piqued accepts a stranger's offer of a sniff of cocaine.

"They say it's an aphrodisiac, Prof," the tempter whispers, "but I wouldn't know about that."

However, all that happens to the Professor is that his nose goes numb. Just as well, as it turns out.

Fifteen minutes pass and Bella remains in the American's arms, revolving like a lamb on a spit. The Professor of Philosophy, despite himself, is increasingly tormented; not only by the actual image of Bella in revolution, but also by the fearful illusion that what is being re-enacted in front of him is nothing less than the deflowering of his own daughter, long imagined. Gradually Bella and his daughter become hopelessly confused in his fogged mind and his resentment toward the American grows from simple jealousy into an insane conviction that he is deliberately mocking his quality as a lover and, worse, as a father. In other words, he feels himself provoked, and already driven thus far it only takes a trick of the light (or is he really kissing Bella?) to make him leap upon the astounded American!

"What are you doing? Vot are you doing, you bloody Yank?" screams the Professor, aiming several blows at the American.

The American, not really grasping what is going on, lashes out in self-defence and connects with the Professor's curved beak. The Professor, still in an uncontrollable fury, grabs Bella, too shocked to move of her own accord, and drags her out of the flat.

Nor do they stop until they reach the Professor's private address. Once inside, with the light on, Bella screams. Not because she is scared, but because the Professor's face is covered with blood.

"What's the matter?" asks the Professor. Thanks to the cocaine, which is acting as a sort of anaesthetic, he does not know that the American's punch has broken his nose.

Bella cleans the Professor's face with a sponge and warm water.

She asks for no explanation, for she has no doubts that the Professor will give one in his own time. Instead, she smooths down his hair. She kisses him on the forehead. Then, humming, she undresses. Face-up on the bed she suddenly realises that the events of the evening have excited her. And the Professor, also carried along by the momentum of the night, finds an erect member in his pants, a single drop glittering at the tip; overwhelmed, seized with joy, he kneels and pushes his penis between Bella's warm and palpy walls.

With a yelp of amazed pleasure Bella clasps the Professor of Philosophy, and wildly out of control thrashes her hips crying, "Fuck me, fuck me, daddy-o!"

His last restraint vanishing with that cry the Professor gives himself over utterly to his grotesque jerks, and with great shudders comes inside Bella at last. He rolls over gasping, his cock glistening, his eyes shining and his cheeks wet from crying.

When Bella returns home, long after everyone is in bed, she creeps straight into Quentin's darkened study and, carefully lighting a safety match, sets fire to all his bridges.

However, at his own house, the Professor of Philosophy is in an entirely different mood; part remorseful, over his behaviour at the party; part terrified by his spectacular return to potency. Bella had misinterpreted his tears as tears of joy, and he hadn't the heart to disabuse her; how could he tell her that he was weeping for shame? For he had suddenly seen, quite clearly, what had caused his impotence. But at least this awareness now gives him the opportunity to regain his freedom, to re-establish the primacy of rationality over desire, to obey his all-powerful sense of duty. So he sits at his desk and writes two letters. The first is a letter of apology to the American. The second is what is called an "anonymous letter". It is addressed to Quentin. It informs him that, for the past year, his wife has been unfaithful. Having completed the task the Professor stands up, a free man.

He feels good.

LE DOCTEUR ENCHAÎNÉ

Ladies and gentlemen, believe me, among a certain type of girl insanity is a status symbol. You know that all men are supposed to be latent homos; well, let me tell you that all women are latent schizophrenics, but don't ask me why. There is the classic case, I could tell you, of the Nordic lass who informed me (I quote): "I am a woman with a beautiful skin like Greta Garbo" — a real walnut if ever I saw one. Incidentally, between you and me, just as girls who have problems about dancing are called "wallflowers", so I call girls who have problems about sex "walnuts" (sex being the only true cause of madness as old father Freud tells us) — but I suppose you guessed that. Anyway, this poor girl honestly believed that because she articulated the sentence it was true. It is my sad duty to inform you, ladies and gentlemen, that she was a bad judge of female form; any resemblance to Greta Garbo was entirely fictional. She had her wish, she was left alone.

However, more frightening are those misguided girls who know who they are but who think that you are someone else. There was once this female loon who grabbed me in a crowded place and called me by an unfamiliar name, as if the name had something intimate to do with me and she had something intimate to do with the same. Both these examples are members of the species *prole* (viz, the dowdies) in the social grouping of the female mad; it is among the *aristos*, of course, that a touch of the moon is a greatly to be desired public grace. When a beautiful lady says "I'm mad" it means (forgive me, ladies) "get in my pants if you can"; and you want to, there's the rub. You see, the combination of madness and beauty is not only a status symbol, it's a damned aphrodisiac — yes, it's all about sex.

And I say, without fear of contradiction, that psychiatrists are prostitutes of the mind. As in days of old when all the rich young men took their French letters of introduction to the family madam, so now the priceless girlies pay their mind doctors for all the experience and the relief they lack; it is a form of self-assurance. Indeed, there is a kind of january flavour to the distinction between self-knowledge and vanity; as if the whole sea of troubles were but the signal for our prosperous magician to calm the waters and thus be able to give the answer to the real question — "Mirror, mirror on the wall, who is the fairest of them all?" — until the brittle ladies become reflections of themselves, and a breed of succubae is let loose upon the world. I predict, if it isn't so already (a dire warning, ladies and gentlemen), that in time to come all the husbands will run mistresses as they now run second cars, and all the wives will keep their medicine men in houses full of cupboard love — oh, it will be a fine time when all the happy families dance around the totem pole. Have I made myself clear? If mad ladies get laid because they are mad and cool walnuts get married too, then the role of our classy call-boy has nothing to do with the recovery of the senses; on the contrary, he teaches girls how to act mad. I ought to know, I'm a sort of lay psychiatrist myself. Just think of the phrases minted for the purpose of amorous description: "madly in love", "wildly in love", "crazy about you", "potty about you", "head-over-heels in love". I am convinced, beyond doubt, that the function of the psychiatrist is to rationalise the unreasonable.

There's madness and madness, ladies and gentlemen, and if my meaning has been taken aright you'll know what kind of insanity I'm talking about. In ascending social order I'm concerned with the slippery slope between delusion and illusion — but you knew that already. Anyhow, just as there's madness and madness, so there are orgasms and orgasms; for the purposes of this history I've divided them into Socratic Orgasms and Biblical Orgasms (SOS & BOS), a division, one might say, contingent upon different meanings of the verb "to know" (viz, in the first instance "man, know thyself", and in the second "Adam knew Eve"). Obviously (referring to my future image of marital bliss) the first O is the domain of the psychiatrist, and the second Ohhhhh is the prerogative of the husband (lucky chap). We psychiatrists are the true heirs of Descartes; not only are we prostitutes of the mind, but we are also the dedicated pimps and panders who convince our clients of their being by having them repeat (and act out) the phrase, *amo ergo sum*. Ladies and gentlemen, you're probably asking yourselves, "O.K., but what's in it for the psychiatrist, does he do it just for the money?" I'll tell you quick enough: psychiatrists ain't normal, we do not choose but are the chosen; we're the eunuchs in the harem, the fools who speak the truth (whatever that is). We play Plato to the lady's Socks. We are the foot that kicks the ball. We deliver the goodies for the boss. Up up and we're away. SOS. Save our souls.

That's right, ladies and gentlemen, this is the history of my castration. Nothing of mine has been chopped off, of course; but I have been cut to the quick just the same. My tender parts have suited me only to tenor parts in the great operatic joke of our *modus vivendi*. Help me! I beg of you, let the mirror crack from side to side, tell the ego to gogo to hell; ladies and gentlemen, join me in libido lib. Liberate my id! By the way, ladies on your couches, have you ever noticed how the word "ego" resembles the male articles: that round e and that round o on either side of the dangling g all coiled up and ready to go? What do you make of that, eh? Your ego is really my id in disguise! Do the both of us a favour, liberate my id! Please! That was an outburst of passion, whether it was genuine or not I cannot tell, though its spontaneity seems suspect to me. Good God! I can't even trust myself, my hands are tied, and that ain't all.

So when did it start? I don't know, I don't know, but perhaps the last entry in my journal (not diary) is relevant: "Sunshine sunny day sunday. A cookoo flew. I met a madman. 'How are your troubles?' he asked. 'They had me certified insane,' he said, 'because I wanted to do something to benefit mankind.' I did not find out what. He wore brown tweeds. As the sun went down Y was miserable, and she asked me to her room. There I was paid the ambivalent compliment of becoming a shoulder to cry on." That's how it ends. Oh, I intended to write up all she confided in me, but I could never face the task. If you like, I'll confess that this manifestation of apparent laziness was but a cover for the appalling fact that I had ceased to be the main character in my own autobiography; I had become a step-brother to the narrators of *The Great Gatsby*, *Le Grand Meaulnes*, and significantly, *The Sun Also Rises* — well, the sun might also rise, but I know what damn well didn't — we were all inoperative voyeurs. Jesus Christ! I know myself inside out — fuck you, Socrates. I just want to stick my dick through the crack in the looking-glass. But no! the word has gone round that psychiatrists have taken the vow of celibacy — fuck that hypocritical oath — as if we were the priests of a new religion; which is what we are, of course. What a combination — a pimp, a priest, and a prostitute — all in one. I think if the whole world were suddenly struck dumb I might begin to enjoy myself. And that, ladies and gentlemen of the jury, is how I came to be found with a bloody knife in my hand.

I don't know what your friends are like, but every so often one of mine goes mad; not stark-staring bonkers of course, but enough to make it noticeable. You know, I am beginning to think that my friends only keep me on as a guide to lead them back into the real world (wherever that is), sometimes I wish that I had given them all a push in the opposite direction. One such friend, on the re-bound from one brick wall or another, managed by judicious dropping of her pants (upon my advice, naturally) to persuade the management of a theatre club to produce her latest pornographic play, *The Sabre-Toothed Cunt,* all about a prick eater — some wit that girl had! I had to go and see the play — this is a statement of fact, not an intimation of reluctance; I assure you, my gentlemen friends, that had you but seen the leading lady you too would have been buzzing around that queen bee's box-office like greedy wasps — so I took with me as a companion a friend even more lately insane than the lamented authoress. How can I best describe the auditorium? If you can imagine those ancient Greek monuments as giant fruit-bowls, then this basement left-over was an up-turned orange crate; we the audience sat on the four sides facing the centre. The play itself (in case you don't read newspapers) con-sisted of a naked girl (absolutely ravishing, as I said) challenging any member (ha ha) or members in the audience to give her an orgasm. The movements of my companion made me feel uncom-fortable; I did not know what was in her mind. I knew that I could arrange a SOS job for the lady now humping on the stage, but I feared that the big BOS coup was beyond my powers — I had been for too long that dispensible part of the double act when three becomes a crowd (now that I think about it, there is an honourable literary tradition of the second fiddler playing to the bass drum, from Holly and Vincey in *She* to Lumière and Garth in the *Daily Mirror*) — yes, folks, I fiddled while my id burned. And the semen fell all around us like tropical rain.

After the performance, during which our heroine accommodated six gentlemen and two ladies without loss of composure, I rose to go and spied another friend escorting a girl whom I recognised. This girl had blue eyes and blonde hair; she carried her head like a rose upon a stalk. I said, "Hello." She said, "Haven't I seen you somewhere before?" I reminded her. She said, "I remember you, you have a nice face, I used to stare at you for hours and think that we would never meet." I said, "We must meet." She said, "Give me your telephone number; I'll call you because I like your face." I was in ecstasies, sat by the telephone for days on end; you see, it doesn't take much to make me happy. Yes, ladies, flattery will get you anywhere. In the meantime I had lunch with our mutual acquaintance; I told him that I was waiting for Z to phone. He laughed, told me that in his opinion she was certifiably insane, offered me some evidence, then went to buy his round of drinks. We were joined by a stranger, a foreign poetess, who informed me that she was divorced, childless, and abandoned by umpteen lovers. My companion wrote down her address. When we were alone he winked at me, "She's mad, you know," he said.

Z telephoned me one week after our unexpected reunion, at eight-thirty in the morning. She was crying. She said that she didn't remember who I was (lose five points), but she thought I must be someone important, for she had my number underlined (score five points). "I'm in trouble," she said, "my lover has kicked me out." "Do you need any help?" I said for the nth time. She said, "Yes," and put down the receiver. She phoned me back in the afternoon. "I've moved," she said. "Are you better?" I asked. She said, "Yes, I saw my doctor this afternoon, he told me that I do not have VD." I said, "Good." She said, "The doctor gave me some sedatives." I said, "Oh." She said, "Would you like to come to a party tonight?" I said, "Yes." She said, "I'll call you when I'm ready to go," and put down the receiver again. She phoned back at midnight, "I decided not to go," she said, "because my friend is too unbalanced to meet anyone new." I said, "Really?" She said,

"Would you like to come to a party tomorrow?" I said, "Yes."
She said, "I'll meet you at the Angel at eight," and put down the
receiver once more. I waited at the Angel station until nine, but she
didn't turn up. When I got home the phone was ringing. It was Z.
"I'm sorry," she said, "but the friend I was visiting had a nervous
breakdown while I was there and when I wanted to leave to meet
you he held me to the floor." I could hear music in the background.
I did not expect to see Z again. But I did, nine weeks later, in a
bookshop; I thought that this meeting was fate (you see what a
fool I am, ladies and gentlemen) and asked her out to dinner.
"Pick me up at my flat," she said.

And now, ladies and gentlemen, we come to the climax of my
sorry tale. On the night in question one of her neighbours let me
into the flat. Z was sitting on her bed; she was wearing a black hat
and a nightdress. Her room was dirty. "My grandfather has gone
mad," she said, "what shall I write to him?" She showed me the
postcard she intended to use; it was a painting of a clown. Then
she got up and said, "I can't eat dinner tonight." She walked
around me and stood in front of the window; the light shone
through and through her nightdress. I could see that she was naked
beneath the transparent gown, and that she had a beautiful body.
She sat down on the edge of the bed, "I've had two men this week,"
she said, "do you want to make it the hattrick?" She pulled her
nightdress up to her navel and opened her legs; oh, indeed, up flew
the web and floated wide, the thighs cracked from side to side. "Do
you like this pose?" she asked, "Charming," I said. She said, "I
went to Soho last week and had some pornographic photographs
taken." I was sitting on a hard chair. We sat in silence. Z went out
of the room and made a telephone call. Suddenly I had a revela-
tion. The girl was clearly sick, a real walnut, a mind in sore need
of the faithful SOS treatment; but her body was so beautiful, it
was a terrible waste, if only I could be her BOS and benefactor too.
But how, ladies and gentlemen? How was I going to rid myself
of the responsibility for her mind, that terrible thing? How was I
to resolve my cartesian dilemma? I looked into her small kitchen, a
cupboard. "Coffee?" she enquired. But before I could answer the
doorbell rang. A man came in. He paid Z some money and began
to undress. He nodded at me. Z took off her nightdress and was

naked. I did not sit still. As the man moved on into Z I slashed him from shoulder to shoulder with a carving knife from the filthy kitchen; it must have been painful for him, but it was not dangerous. I held the knife to his throat and ordered him to tie Z to the bed, then I told him to go. I knelt on Z's chest so that she had to gasp for breath, and while her mouth was wide open I cut out her tongue. It wasn't easy, ladies and gentlemen, believe me; Z thrashed about so much that I thought she must be having an orgasm. Then she began to gurgle, so I cut her loose and sat her up. I was ready to take her, or so I thought, but when I came to check the famous equipment I saw, to my astonishment, that I had already come, and realised that I must have shot my bolt while slicing her tongue. I knelt at her feet, at this discovery, and began to stroke her belly. She was shivering. I pressed my face against her body, and took one of her nipples between my lips. And I sucked and sucked while she sat silent and still with blood pouring out of her mouth and on to my hair.

And that, ladies and gentlemen of the jury, is how the police found us when they burst in. The judge has called my crime the most horrible he has come across in all his years on the bench. And I readily admit that I have done wrong in his eyes, but who among you can blame me? In fact, ladies and gentlemen, I believe that my unorthodox treatment has at last enabled Z to come to terms with herself, certainly she is now more beautiful than ever. The questions you must decide, ladies and gentlemen, are whether I was more sinned against than sinning, and whether, in the final analysis, I did more good than harm. If you don't believe me, ask Z.

TANTE ROUGE

My toothbrush has four blue scores behind its head that look as if they had been made by a cat's paw dipped in ink, only explicable if their presence is gratuitous. My toothbrush is a long white bone and I keep it in a perspex box, at present it is in the bathroom of Sylvie's aunt. *Quelle chambre!* (as they say in France): ultramarine bath the size of an aquarium, tiles as rosy as an ears' conch, recorded sea sounds, water as limitless as the unconscious, which place is where I was when Sylvie woke me with a scream. Unusual, because I do not usually sleep later than my ladies, perhaps because I wish to preserve my ubiquity, like the Cheshire Cat. Well, there is not much going through the looking-glass when you are awake, so even though our vast bed was as comfortable as a pacific ocean, I opened a blue eye and observed that Sylvie was peeping through the winter window. Her unclothed pale skin was slightly flushed from the cold, the shade of a blushing carnation, though I must say what I first thought of when I saw her standing in her goose pimples was my old pinkish ping-pong bat. Incompatible images? However, I had a more important question to answer, namely, why was Sylvie screaming? I noticed in addition, as I considered the possible causes, an antiphony that came from beyond the window, something like *skyow skyou*, a feathered echo of her plaintive cry. Such was the dawn chorus that morning.

"*Regarde*," exclaimed Sylvie as soon as I was close, "*le lac!*"

I should explain. Sylvie and I were temporary residents at the mansion of her aunt, the famed Tante Rouge. Commie and divorcée as may be, the aunt was still an aristocrat, therefore in her gardens there was a lake. The lake was a gem, a sparkling jewel in the over-dressed park, ruby red, full of nourishing dye to keep the flamingoes in fiery plumage. The aunt, you see, collected flamingoes, an exotic hobby, far more difficult and dignified than breeding peacocks. Anyway, it being a cold winter morning following a frosty night, the priceless water had turned icy, and a prize flamingo, sleeping late, had been trapped by its feet in the frozen pond. It struggled to get free, wings as red as my Sylvie's cheeks, but its flames didn't cut any ice with Jack Frost. Furthermore, to make matters worse for the poor bird, Sylvie's aunt's handsome Persian puss (Le Chat de Perse, Pliny thought its whiteness came from eating snow), was creeping carefully over the glazed lake towards its frightened and frantic breakfast. The bird screeched in terror, *skyow skyou skyoooooooooow!*

"Oh, *mon Dieu!*" wailed Sylvie. "Save it!" *Skyow skyou!*

I am ready to admit that there are many people in this world with a more cheerful disposition than me the first thing in the morning, however, Le Chat de Perse was not one of them. Natural history experts and cat lovers both are perhaps aware of this fact already, that autocratic cats do not take kindly to being prevented from enjoying their chosen meal. Consequently, as I pushed the furry beast away from its all but extinguished prey, Persius lashed out a white paw in fury and with claws as sinister as its national scimitar left four red lines on the back of my right hand. I jumped away in surprise and pain, a natural mistake, as a result of which I lost my delicate footing on the thin ice; for a few seconds I juggled with my feet to keep my balance, but it wasn't any use, and I tumbled backwards. If the same thing has happened to you, or if you are perchance an Eskimo, you will know that the sound of cracking ice is quite unmistakable; I broke up the lake all right; splits raced outwards from my gaping hole like ripples of frozen laughter. I spluttered, splashed, and shivered, my body contracted as if to prevent the appalling water from entering my pores, I squirmed, and swam, and all the while in the background to this bubbling cacophony I imagined I could hear icicles of glacial giggling. There is nothing at all dignified in drowning. As for the flamingo, the *sine qua non* of my unenviable plight, it hopped away without so much as a *skyou*, let alone a thank you. I hope it gets chilblains.

"Is it permanent, do you think?" I asked, examining my hands, which had turned scarlet.

My face was scarlet too, and there were stains of a lighter red on various portions of my anatomy where the dye had seeped through my discarded clothing, all in all I looked like a man caught in a state of peculiar embarrassment. Sylvia rubbed my numb body with a prickly towel, the texture and size of a schooner's main sail; I gather that only the very rich can afford such Spartan luxuries.

"You must not worry," began Sylvie with relish, "it stays only on flamingoes, *mais jusqu'à tu es comme d'habitude* (laughter) you should keep away from the lady flamingoes, it would not be fair to them."

I was not amused. For years flamingoes did not breed in captivity, until some bright spark realised that the mature birds required their alluring pigmentation, somehow lost by the waters of Babylon, to remind them to perform coitus, up to then a faded figment of the collective instinct. So the word went around among the cognoscenti; turn 'em red, and watch 'em go. I was a victim of this advance in scientific knowledge.

Sylvie threw the towel to the winds and hugged me, the next stage in my rehabilitation, she whispered in my ear, *"Je comprends le goût de madame le flamant,"* meaning red hands and a red face drive a girl wild, a further scientific advance it seems.

So we kissed, and I got a little warmer, until sensations began to reappear over my body like coordinates on an ordnance survey map.

"Attende!" hissed Sylvie as she attempted to attract the attention of my frigid cock (but as I said, my whole body had contracted in the drink), and my south pole appeared to want to remain *pays inconnu.* "Attende!"

Patience is a virtue. Sylvie returned from the mediterranean bathroom decked out like some quattrocento goddess of love in rouges and perfumes. She was of course as naked as a sea nymph. In her hand she held, not a magic wand, but a tube of toothpaste. She unscrewed the top, as though she were some artist preparing for a day's work, and squeezed a white wriggling worm on to my ice cap. Then she rubbed some more of the paste into that place where I believe my foreskin would have been had I not been a member of the chosen race.

"I cannot resist the peppermint flavour," said Sylvie as she came down on me on that soft eiderdown for the third time, some artist!

"Well, well, well," I thought as the warm winds blew, "fellatio!"

"In the summer I make pedalo on that lake," reminisced Sylvie when we were back in her flat, away from the mansion of La Tante Rouge (fellow traveller, first class), back to the potato-seller downstairs, the wine merchant across the street, back to the ghetto in the fourth arrondissement, where corks bob all winter in the rainwater that runs along the gutters. Sylvie told me that.

I first met her in the autumn by design. "Would you mind delivering a letter?" I had been asked by a fellow Francophile who was crossing La Manche in the opposite direction. "It is to a girl who lives in Paris." And that is how Sylvie became this theme played on a name and an address. There is no postmark on the letter, so the exact date of my entry into Sylvie's life is not a recorded fact, nothing was registered, I simply enquired of the potato-seller and part-time concierge *pour l'étage juste*.

"*Petites patates*," replied the dirty old man with a chip on his shoulder, "*petites patates*."

"*Pourquoi?*" asked a customer who got the dusty joke.

"Because I have a French letter for someone," I answered.

The stairs inside were wooden and worn, wedded to a shiny banister that twisted upward into the centre of the ancient building like a corkscrew into a bottle of wine. Sylvie dwelt by the more untrodden ways, the sixth floor, where the sky touched the roof, so high that I was dizzy by the time that I tapped on her door. This is the only excuse I can give to explain how it was that I walked into her bathroom by mistake and saw Sylvie sitting in the tub soaping herself.

"*Qui êtes vous?*" demanded Sylvie as suds slipped all over her shiny body and drips dripped from her nipples.

"*Le facteur*," I said, holding out the letter as if it were a laissez-passer or a passport into personal chambers, which is what it turned out to be in effect.

Sylvie took the letter from my hand in a way which made my presence seem to be nothing out of the ordinary, presumably convinced by the evidence of my blushing visage that I was no malefactor, and proceeded to study the handwriting on the envelope.

"Is it true," she asked, "that all English men are very shy?"

I had no answer to that. She dropped the letter into the water where it floated undisturbed until she got out of the bath, at which point the envelope stuck to her wet back. I could still read her name and address very clearly, just above her private mail box. As a result of this encounter we spent the autumn, as the French say, looking at leaves upsidedown. I have my memories too. Writers do not meet many girls like Sylvie.

And who is Sylvie? I have looked at her and have seen the way cheeky dimples sneak into her face when she smiles, the way pimples rise on the coral aureola of her breast when she is aroused, have felt the way she scratches my back with ferocious fingernails like diamonds from a pack of cards. Right now, in this kitchen, her hair is pulled back in a bun, after the fashion of the peasants of Northern France, showing off the roundness of her face. Her eyes are as dark as chocolate. Her skin is as fine as sifted flour. She has been baking a cake.

"What are you thinking?" she asks. "Why do you smile?"

There in a couple of questions you have the difference between us; Sylvie wonders what goes on in my head, while I watch for the idiosyncrasies that will characterise her. Oscar Wilde proclaimed somewhere or other that it is a shallow man who does not judge by appearances, and I hope he is right, yet I cannot help but sometimes feel like an ornithologist who knows he has seen a golden oriole by its bright yellow plumage, its black wings, and the dark bar on its tail. Is Sylvie simply a common girl (*femina femina vulga*) with regulation mammary glands, a black bush beneath her belly button, and labia between her legs, or is it just my imagination that makes her a unique specimen who opens her thighs for me not merely because I tend to have red hands and a red face, but also because she feels an ulterior motive which we shall not embarrass by naming? And what do I feel? Ah, now we are on the horns of my paradox; I should like to know Sylvie, in the same way as I want Sylvie to desire and know me, yet I can only respond to her decorations (natural and unnatural). When she embroiders herself for me, it is the image that I (as the French put it) *baiser*.

"*Imbécile!*" yells Sylvie. "*Imbécile!* have you lost your sense of smell?" The abuse was well deserved, the great writer had burnt the cake.

Though the gâteau was a chocolate affair the top was too tanned to contemplate with any appetite, even after I had swept it with such cutting strokes that cinders flew like sand in a desert storm. We had a cake but we couldn't eat it.

"*Bouffon!*" mocked Sylvie. "See what you have done!"

"Wait," I commanded, "and watch what I will do, just wait!"

With purposeful strides towards the table I began the transformation scene, spread out all the ingredients I would require, washed my hands, wiped them on a white towel, and set to work. I broke a three-ounce block of plain chocolate into small pieces, placed them in a copper pan where water already waited, and allowed the thickening combination to mingle over a gentle heat. As soon as the contents began to boil I turned off the gas, let the mixture cool till all the brown bubbles stopped breathing, and beat in fine icing-sugar (a spoonful at a time), salad oil, and three drops of vanilla essence. While this concoction warmed on the stove I searched Sylvie's cupboards for what I wanted; a forcing bag and a set of icing pipes. And so the moment arrived when I turned the bitter ashes into sweetness itself, as I slowly spread the rich icing over the cake.

"*Voilà!*" I cried in triumph. I waved sticky fingers, dipped in the gluey chocolate, beneath Sylvie's sensitive nostrils, they flared (*narines flambées*), and a hot tongue slipped through moist lips to languorously lick my fingers clean.

"*O monsieur,*" she gasped, "*tu es un génie.*"

However, I was not finished yet; as a preface to the climax of my act I fitted a writing pipe to the tip of the forcing bag and poured in the remainder of the chocolate glacé. I squeezed the fat bag with tender care, so that I was almost caressing it, and Sylvie watched open-mouthed as I manoeuvred the flowing line into the alphabetical shape of an ornamental dedication. It was a masterpiece. And, what is more, I had discovered a new aphrodisiac. We made a lot of chocolate icing that winter, enough to coat a body many times over, those sweetmeat sessions. Oh, you with the liquorice lips, say you will be mine.

Is it true what they sing, those songs about Paris, so romantic, rhapsodic, is it the capital city of Wonderland, where real feelings burst into imaginary blossom at the drop of an awakening note?

I'll never know, because I woke too soon, but what a musical winter we had, Sylvie and I. We hibernated. Grew together in Sylvie's fertile flat, her gracious gynaeceum entertained my stamen in all manner of arrangements, hypogynous, perigynous, and epigynous, and my rapacious stamen entered her gynaeceum through the anterior lobes and the posterior lobes, the upper lips and the lower lips, we made love like the crocus and the lotus, until we had been through every flower in the perfumed garden. We played all the tunes known to Pan's pipes. We sought to improve upon nature's schemes, borrowed colour techniques from great painters, and rhythms from famous composers, but after my polychrome can had watered her lavender labia for the umpteenth time I knew that our culture was at an impasse. I had grown impatient with impasto, my fingers itched to touch what my eye could see, and soft sfumato no longer sufficed to excite me. I wanted to taste the voluptuous veal that hid behind the veil. So temperate Sylvie has turned to the ways of bright tempera. She sits silent, cross-legged on sofa cushions, breaking eggs. The music comes from the one-eyed box where Sam plays a tune, while old lovers meet, and bare trees bloom in Memory Forest, then there is a flashback to those former times beneath Paris's pleasure dome. What do you say, Sam?

"You must remember this, a kiss is still a kiss, a sigh is just a sigh;

The fundamental things apply, as time goes by."

With my other eye I watch Sylvie skilfully separate the yolks from the whites, and roll the viscous balls across the palms of her hands. One such ball, more adventurous than most, escapes and slides down her belly to explode over her curly roots, making them clammy and glutinous and quite irresistible, oh how those thick drips between the thighs made my umbrella rise! The rest of the sacs are punctured, not by my hydrophobic desires, but by Sylvie with a silver pin. Pigments made with hues from natural earth are mixed in with mother hen's yellows and the paints are ready for use.

"*Quelles couleurs, aujourd'hui?*" asks Sylvie, an impossible question.

"A hint of rose madder on the bosom drives me to distraction, and raw sienna under the arms is a blow below the belt," I explain. "Perhaps you could try a little burnt umber on the buttocks for the monkey glands, and violet anywhere, oh, it isn't fair." And I give up.

Sylvie wets the sable brush, browses over the eyes, and descends to the body, adding layers of translucent tones until the semi-opaque colour shines on her skin with a luminous light, and I adore my apricot mademoiselle; but oh my illuminated Sylvie, why did we go out?

"She likes to meet writers," Sylvie said, "how do you say? because it puts another feather in her cap?"

"That's right." I had asked why it was that her aunt had invited me to the château for dinner. It was an unusually warm day, a rare day, and there was a distinctly Parisian pleasure in sitting at an open table in one of the local pavement cafés sipping coffee and eating croissants. Sylvie was wearing a low-cut black dress that made her breasts seem like a pair of crescent moons shining in the night. A necklace of expensive diamond, tourmaline, amethyst, and aquamarine sparkled at her throat like the aurora borealis; she looked very glamorous. Her long fingers, so well known to me for a variety of services, were concealed beneath silky evening gloves. The waiter who served us was a chic fellow, he didn't so much as bat a mascara eyelid at Sylvie's outfit, but to me it seemed that Sylvie was sporting the uniform of an exclusive society to which I did not belong. My own suit and tie made me feel earthbound, I could not match Sylvie's astronomical elegance.

"*Vingt francs*," demanded the effeminate garçon, who affected a look of surprise when I paid the bill.

Sylvie took my arm as we strolled down the Rue de Rivoli and through the Jardin des Tuileries in the afternoon sunshine of that false spring day, followed all the while by the intimate ghosts of our shadows. (There is no élitism among shadows, all shadows are equal.) We walked a little way along the banks of the Seine, where contented fishermen sat among their straw hampers and bottles of *vin ordinaire* waiting for the *goujons*, following the curve of the river until we stood opposite the Tour Eiffel. As we watched the sun caught the spray from the fountains and created a momentary rainbow, as if the day were not already vainglorious enough. It was splendid.

"Paris can be very beautiful," murmured Sylvie, catching the tune of my familiar continental mermaid, catching an echo of my own thoughts. But at our backs, on the Avenue de Versailles, the traffic honked and hooted like a ravenous pack of diurnal predators. "Come, let us go," said Sylvie, "we must not be late." A taxi took us to our destination, *la maison de sa tante*, midway between Paris and Versailles. I noticed as we pushed our way through the thick ivy to reach the dangling bell that there were sleepy hedgehogs crawling over lawns as unnaturally green as emeralds. It seems that mother nature has got as many tricks up her sleeve as any artist, the old cheat.

As befits an aristocrat of her political colour, Sylvie's aunt did not keep servants, instead our meal was served by male and female mannequins liberated from the house of the most exhalted haut couturier in Paris. The girl who poured me extravagant glasses of wine was a beauty of flawless perfection, so much so that when she stood still it was difficult to believe that she was real, an illusion emphasised by the facts that she neither spoke nor even smiled. Not so Sylvie's aunt.

"My niece," she confided to me midway through the second course, "has a heart like an artichoke." And so saying she took another petal of that vegetable and scooped out the flavoured flesh with a pair of dazzling incisors.

"That is not polite, Auntie!" interrupted Sylvie. "*Tu n'es pas gentille.*"

"*Oui, monsieur,*" continued the aunt polishing off another petal, "guard your emotions, Sylvie is not a constant lover, she likes variety."

"You talk so much, *ma tante,*" chided Sylvie wagging an extraneous silver fork, "that you have neglected to ask our guest if he is enjoying his food."

"*Pardon, tu as raison.* Are you?" she asked.

"Very much, thank you," I replied, though in truth the first course, called Potage d'Hérisson, a heavily spiced soup which could not quite conceal the taste of privet hedges, was not entirely successful.

The plates were cleared by our silent helpers, and the star of the banquet was carried in on an oval platter that shone with the reflected light of the congregation of candles; not to be outdone, the main course itself burned with a blue flame as very special cognac evaporated into the air. A roasted breast was placed daintily on my plate by hands that were as graceful and quick as a bird. I cut a slice and tasted the dish, it was more delicate by far than any wild duck, I could almost hear the applause and cries of encore in my stomach for this gastronomic hit.

"It is magnificent," I complimented my hostess. "Now tell me what I am eating."

"I thought that you would like it," the proud lady said, "we call it Filet de Flamant Flambée."

"You eat your flamingoes?" I was astonished.

"In France we have a saying, monsieur," Sylvie's aunt began grandily, "*s'il mouvoit on le mange*; if it moves, eat it. Why else should one keep flamingoes, may I ask?"

I now understood the ingratitude of the flamingo I had saved; to it I was just another flamingo-eater. I felt guilty for my kind.

"*Et maintenant, mes amis*," announced our elegant MC, our mistress of ceremonies, "*nous allons à la chambre des pieuvres.*"

So Sylvie and I quit the scene of our feast and followed La Tante Rouge down a flight of filigree steps, in and out of a labyrinth of passages, and through an oaken door into a dark room suffused with the saline smell of the sea. We both still held in our hands, as though I were Atlas and she my helpmate, two hemispheres stuffed full of ice-cream, hot morello cherries, and cake.

"You must be very flattered, my aunt has honoured you," whispered Sylvie as she fed me spoonfuls of the bitter-sweet desert. "Not many persons have been here before you."

Slowly waves of blue-green light filtered into the chamber and I saw simultaneously that one of the walls was constructed of glass and that the world beyond was not made of air but of water.

"Ah, *c'est merveilleux, mon vieux*," said Sylvie's aunt, "they are coming, monsieur, and now you are going to witness something very special."

I certainly did. From out of a sandy nook or cranny at the base of that very private aquarium an octopus emerged, its movements surprisingly delicate, like the disembodied hands of a famous artist, with no hint of the strangler of the sailors' shanties. At the entrance of a second octopus from the shadowy wings the first turned as white as a tutu and stood upon tiptoe moving towards the new-comer like a ballet dancer on points.

"Once I watched him execute an exquisite *entrechat*," said Sylvie's aunt.

"A duet of lovers is a beautiful thing," added Sylvie, still feeding me ice-cream and cake.

However, the female of the species was not nearly as impressed as the audience, probably because she had seen better performances in the proper ocean, and paid no attention to her partner even as he approached her with the third tentacle on his right side fully erect and aiming in her direction. But the male was no mere sucker either, he too must have had better times and still had a trick or two up his sleeve; he covered his body with stripes of black and white, managed an energetic pirouette, and swung back like a compass pointing at his lady friend, who must have found this display of foreplay quite irresistible because she joined her mate in the famous *pas de deux* which ended in his stiff limb sticking into an orifice in her rear *tout de suite*. Very soon a seam beneath the straight arm began to undulate from him to her, but before the grand finale could be reached Sylvie's aunt (who should have known better) burst into spontaneous raptures and put the male lead right off his stroke. Indeed, so alarmed was the poor fellow that he squirted ink all over the place instead, so that the water became full of black clouds and nothing more was visible.

"Never mind, *n'importe*," said Sylvie's aunt, "it is time for the entertainments, anyway."

The cabaret was another surprise. The five male and the five female mannequins, each pair apparently a replica of a prototype concealed deep in the vaults of a Paris bank, returned from the kitchens and removed their identical costumes with a series of gestures that must have been copied from an obscure choreography. The rest of their performance was more ordinary; the men fucked the women. However, I soon found that I was not enjoying myself, any more than I would have gained pleasure from seeing the couple in Jan Van Eyck's famous canvas strip down and get on with the job of sharing out their conjugal rights. Not only was the spectacle unerotic at heart, it also devalued the worth of my own antics between the sheets with Sylvie, like any miser with his money I have always believed that things are more valuable when examined in the privacy of the bedroom (or whichever room is handy). It is a great problem, for this artist at any rate, to come to terms with the realisation that he is not unique, not the first nor the last. I had just begun to consider my own role in the proceedings when Sylvie stood up.

"Would you please unclasp my necklace?" she asked. Her gloves, dress, shoes, and lingerie followed her jewellery to the floor, in that order; it turned out that my Sylvie was an experienced stripper.

I did what was expected of me up to the sticking point, but could do no more, when it came to the moment of truth I was as limp as a drowning man amid that sea of humping bums. Alone with Sylvie I had always managed to counterfeit the impression that what we were doing was somehow an original breakthrough in the intimate relations between man and woman, now I was confronted with five separate sets of proof that my coin was not so special; result, no ink in the pen.

"It is useless, Sylvie," I confessed, "I would never be able to write in front of an audience, so how can you expect me to make love in public?"

"Do not be alarmed; it happens to everyone the first time," called Sylvie's aunt across the room. "Put on your clothes and come here, I have a souvenir for you." My old enemy, Le Chat de Perse, sat on her lap lace, it may only have been my mood, but it seemed to me that there was an unmistakable look of triumph in its inscrutable eyes. The present was a long pink feather, with grateful thanks from the late flamingo.

There is a lot that a man and a woman alone together can do with a feather; for example, I know the exact location of every spot on Sylvie's body where she is most ticklish, a tempting invitation to the fandango if ever there was one. Sylvie hadn't bothered to remove her clothes from the dining-room, and at this moment she is prone upon the bed in a classic pose, *in puris naturalibus*, her Pandora's box open wide, letting the world know all the little secrets of *femina femina vulga*. And myself? Despite the pulsating ache situated in the region of my groin that represents the time-honoured desire to fill her carnal knowledge with my own store of wisdom, I am seated at a table dipping my quill into a black inkwell. It is my conclusion that literature must transcend the stale pleasures of the flesh if it is to become a useful guide into the country of fresh excess, or else the writer will finish his career as a mere mime-artist grinding out an infinite procession of bumps in the night. That's right, I want to be the Natty Bumppo of sexual experience, diviner of dark delights, not just another gigolo.

"Come to me," Sylvie calls, "come to me, *j'ai faim, j'ai soif, j'ai besoin de toi.*"

Au revoir, Sylvie, I've been there before, so long, Sylvie, your paint is fading fast. The four scars on the back of my hand throb as I write, but I've got to set out for the territory ahead of the rest. In the end it comes to this, the pen is mightier than the penis! What do you say, Sam?

HEARTS OF GOLD

There are not many happy families. Not among the rich. You soon learn that in my line of business. So why was I down? I wasn't rich and I had no family. It was one of those oppressive days when you feel like you've been trapped in a kitchen by a homicidal cook who's frying burgers and onions in gasoline. A regular Los Angeles summer day. But there was something more nagging me. The knock on the door reminded me what it was. Mrs Virginia Lyle walked in. My client. Her perfume was the sort you smell in wet dreams. She looked like a second-rate opera singer, but then I was a second-rate private eye, so we suited each other just fine.

"Have you brought the letter?" I said.

"Right here," she said, patting her purse.

"I still don't know why you don't mail it," I said, "this'll cost more than a thirteen cent stamp."

"Listen, Mr Smolinsky, I've mailed a dozen letters and they've all come back marked 'return to sender'," said Mrs Lyle, "this one I want to be sure Laura gets."

"How will I find your daughter?" I said.

"I don't know her address," said Mrs Lyle, "but she dances every night with Jackettes at Mikel Ratskin's joint on the Strip at Vegas."

"O.K.," I said.

"One more thing, Mr Smolinsky," said Mrs Lyle, "wait while Laura reads the letter, I want to know her reaction."

When she was gone I opened my window to be rid of her fragrance, it kept reminding me of my status as a messenger boy for retired whores. No use. It clung to my clothes for hours.

I drove non-stop to Las Vegas in my old Volkswagen. The desert sky was turning emerald green as I arrived, a beauty unremarked by the inhabitants. I toured around a bit before I finally checked into a cheap motel built on the outskirts of the city beside a road-sign which read: "Leave Paradise, enter Winchester." The motel, forming a rebus from Paradise, called itself the Pair of Dice. The air-conditioning in my room didn't work, making it hotter than hell inside. It was too early to look up Laura. So I put on a jacket and tie and went to dine at Howard Johnsons, which also served breakfast twenty-four hours a day. The doorman was a former cop. He was still wearing a gun. I ordered a steak, other people were eating eggs, for them the day was just beginning. You could see the man at the next table had just got up. He was combing his grey hair and patting down the sides with his hands. His pink shirt was open to the *pupik* and he wore a gold medallion around his neck. Life had given him a thirty-year head start on his latest wife who had yellow hair that was whipped up like a piece of confectionery. When the waiter brought their breakfast the man squeezed his wife's breasts like they were oranges.

"Hey, Franco, what is a fifty-five-year-old guy doing with a wife with such firm tits?" he said. "Franco, Franco, you should have seen her last night in her red dress — what a number! — I swear she drove twenty men bananas — at least!" The golden charm palpitated on his hairy chest.

In the corner by the pay-phone a drunk in a mohair suit was blubbering down the receiver, "You're my favourite granddaughter, sweetheart, you know how the song goes, 'My one and only'."

I paid my check. On the streets things were no better. A giggling group of greaseballs tumbled out of the Lady Luck Wedding Chapel, which also offered wedding suites bookable by the hour, yelling, "Give it to her, Billy-boy!" Then on the Strip itself where low-life habits were transformed by electricity into glamorous pursuits, as the neon lights burned the sky, eclipsing the stars and turning night to noon. And the biggest lights shone for Ratskin's "Palace of the Princess".

I stood by the bar and ordered a whisky sour. The place was crowded with smart folk, for the Jackettes were the hottest thing in town. Wild rumours circulated about their origins; some said that Ratskin had trained them with lumber jacks in the days when he controlled the wood and paper rackets. Certainly the girls were all giantesses. They seemed so much larger than life as they strutted out onto the tiny stage in their jackboots and their birthday suits. Laura Lyle was at their head, the only blonde in the troupe. Their bodies were oiled and the sweat rolled down and splashed while they undulated to the sound of bongos, flickering through the spotlights like vamps from a 3-D nightmare. The audience hushed as they began to dance round a male mannequin, faster and faster, till they were the puppets of the drumbeats; then spinning, sweating, these naked savages picked up axes and as the silver heads flashed hacked the wax model to pieces. When it was quiet the audience went wild. I tried to get backstage. The doorman blocked my way.

"Take it easy, mister," he said, "ain't no one allowed back there."

I took out my cheque book. "How much will it cost?" I said.

"Cheques are bad news," he said, "can't bank 'em 'cos bribes are non-deductable. Bring me one hundred dollars cash tomorrow night and I'll see what I can do."

Which meant another night in Las Vegas.

The Bank of Nevada still had Nixon's official inauguration patch hanging on its wall. Underneath ran this legend, "January 20 1973, Richard M. Nixon, President of the United States, resigned August 9 1974. Spiro T. Agnew, Vice-President of the United States, resigned October 10 1973." Not the sort of pair you'd want to be reminded of, especially in a bank. But this was Las Vegas. The air might be cleaner than Los Angeles, but that just made the smell of corruption more sickly-sweet; it stuck to you like the lacquer the women used to protect their permanent waves from the desert wind. I got my money and spent the rest of the day beside the cool blue pool, watching couples move silently from their autos to their motel rooms as if their thoughts were too dirty for the open air. I decided to catch Laura before the show, so when the sky began to turn lemon I buttoned my shirt and walked up the Strip toward the Palace of the Princess. The wind had blown up during the afternoon displacing many letters from the sign that spelt out JACKETTES so men now ran up and down ladders carrying them on their backs. The doorman remembered me. I gave him his hundred dollars. Laura Lyle was alone in the dressing-room, naked from the waist down. Her legs were long and brown, like life-size swizzle sticks. She was dusting her pubic hair with silver powder so as to match her dyed head.

She looked at me and said, "Whatever you offer won't be enough, I don't screw with shmucks."

I smiled. "I'm a private detective," I said, "I've come to deliver a letter."

"Alright, mister mailman," she said, "let's see it."

I handed her Virginia's letter. She opened it and snorted.

"Any message?" I said.

"Yes," said Laura, "tell the old bitch to go fuck herself with a zucchini."

That seemed to be the end of that. Beyond the dressing-room I could hear the sound of axes hitting wood; the Jackettes were practising for the night's performance.

Outside the doorman was waiting for me. "The boss wants to see you," he said. He was holding a gun.

Mikel Ratskin was once a famous man. In the days when he controlled the paper supply every newspaper syndicate depended upon his goodwill to keep going. Sycophants wrote biographies. Nightclub comedians invented jokes about him. Politicians were photographed in his company. What finally blew Mikel's empire apart was a glut of cheap paper from Eastern Europe followed immediately by a clutch of accusations in the press. So Mikel gathered his family and his possessions and retired to Las Vegas. His business actitivies might have been gangsterish but his private life was blameless; he remained faithful to his wife and he doted on his little daughter. Ratskin was smaller than I expected. I wondered what he could want with me.

"Listen, son," he said, "are you going to tell me why you wanted to see Laura so much?"

There was no harm in him knowing, so I told him about Virginia's letter.

At which he grunted with laughter. "My boy," he said, "do you have any idea what was in that letter? Well, I'll tell you. Virginia Lyle has run a couple of cat houses on Sunset Boulevard for years, these days they've got fancy names like the 'Institute of Oral Love' and the 'Participating Center of Sexual Experience'. But the service is still the same. Now get this. Laura, her one daughter, turned out to be the best hooker she ever had and the customers keep asking for her, so Virgina — that's Laura's *mother* — keeps begging her to come home. To fuck strangers for money!"

"I don't think Laura will be going," I said.

"Of course not," said Ratskin. "Laura's a sweet kid. In fact Mr—"

"Smolinsky."

"—Mr Smolinsky, she's my daughter's companion. That's really why I asked for you to come to my office. We get all kinds of kooks trying to get to Princess through Laura. You can't be too careful."

He looked at me sharply, as if he were trying to judge my character with a single glance.

"Sit down, Mr Smolinsky," he said at last, "I've decided to take you into my confidence. You are a Jewish private detective. *Nu?* So you understand how important is a family. Well, Mr Smolinsky, until recently I thought I had a happy home. Now I'm not so sure. To tell you the truth, Mr Smolinsky, I think someone is *shtupping* my wife." He rose from his desk, upon which stood an antique telephone and an enlargement of his family, and walked to where I sat. He put his arm around my shoulder. "Everything I have done has been for my family," he said, "my wife, my daughter and my future son-in-law. I don't want to see it all go to nothing. Help me, Mr Smolinsky." His arms tightened. "Find the son-of-a-bitch who's *shtupping* my wife!"

"Mr Ratskin," I said, "have you any proof that this lover exists?"

"Proof!" he shouted, "proof! It's your job to find proof. I just need suspicions."

I took the job.

"Wonderful," said Ratskin, "now come back and meet the family. Have dinner with us."

Mikel Ratskin's house was modest for someone with more money than the average European treasury. As he opened the front door a girl flung herself into his arms.

"Poppa!" she cried.

Mikel laughed and patted her head. Around her neck the word PRINCESS dangled like a charm from a golden chain. Above the letter "I" was a tiny mogen david.

"Princess," said Ratskin, "I want you to meet Mr Smolinsky."

"Hi," she said.

She was a beauty. Her hair was chestnut red. Her eyes were brown. I was not in her class. I belonged in the B-movie with the Las Vegas background along with the likes of Virginia and Laura Lyle. Ratskin, too, despite his wealth and the patina of refinement that went with it was still a B-movie mobster. But he had achieved one of his ambitions at least, his daughter was of better quality than he or his wife could ever be. And didn't Anna Ratskin know it. The looks she gave Princess were full of envy.

We dined on artichokes and fresh salmon. Princess had a voluptuous way with artichokes; she pulled off each leaf as if she were undressing the vegetable, then she dipped it in the hot butter sauce and slid it in and out of her mouth like she had learned to eat the thing at the Institute of Oral Love. Rivulets of butter overflowed her lower lip and filled the dimple in her chin. When she reached the centre of the artichoke she pushed her finger between the silver hairs and pulled apart the purple lips to reveal the soft green heart within. The salmon came fresh and pink as though blushing with its nakedness. Its flesh was soft and sweet. When the meal was over, Anna rose.

"Please excuse me, Mr Smolinsky," she said, "I have to pack a few things. Mikel, I've decided to spend a few days at the house in Furnace Creek."

"Stay as long as you like, my dear," he said, "Princess and I can manage on our own." Ratskin looked at me. I knew what the look meant. His eyes were full of tears.

I drove back to Los Angeles that night. On the seat beside me was a gift from Mikel Ratskin, a globe artichoke of some size and weight. I promised it to myself for a late supper. But first I had to make a stop at the Institute of Oral Love. I had a message for Virginia Lyle. I left the Volkswagen in a parking lot and strolled along Sunset Boulevard looking for the place. A black kid in a tuxedo several sizes too large danced alongside me holding a pumpkin pie.

"Friend," he said, "you don't hate Negroes, do you? I'm selling pumpkin pies for the Muhammad Ali Muslim Project. To help the black kids in Watts. See that man over there, he don't hate

Negroes, he just gave fifty dollars."

I said, "I'll give you a dollar if you can tell me where I'll find the Institute of Oral Love."

Outside the Institute the cops had nothing better to do than tow away a car parked in front of a fire hydrant; its registration plate said, I NEED U. Inside a dusky girl said, "Hi, I'm Laila Tov, from Israel."

I said, "I'm Joshua Smolinsky from Smolensk. I want to see Virginia."

Virginia Lyle sat at a pink desk in a room with pink walls and a deep pink carpet on the floor that looked like a tongue. "Did you give her the letter?" she said.

"Yes," I said.

"Any message?" she said.

I said, "Laura said you should go fuck yourself with a zucchini."

Back in my own apartment I plopped the artichoke into boiling water. Later, when I peeled off the leaves I imagined I was undressing Princess, more and more came off until there was a pile of her clothes around the plate and she was naked; then I began to probe the heart and I knew that something was wrong for the heart was as hard as a rock. I parted the fur and petals and saw in place of the green heart a nugget of gold.

Fairfax Avenue could as well be a street in Tel Aviv with its Hebrew signs swinging in the morning breeze. But the shop in Farmers Market selling yamulkas for dogs could only be in Los Angeles. The stalls in Farmers Market were full of wonderful fruits and vegetables; peaches, plums, grapes, nectarines, cherries, apples, tomatoes, all glowing red, oranges and grapefruit shining like suns and moons, cucumbers, squashes, even zucchinis but not an artichoke to be seen. I asked one of the stallholders why there were no artichokes.

"Don't ask me," he said, "ask the people in Castroville — the so-called Artichoke Capital of the World — they say they haven't got any for us. According to them the entire crop is earmarked for export." I guessed that I was uncovering the beginning of one of Mikel Ratskin's grand designs. But where did I fit in? I didn't know the answer so I ordered some cheese blintzes.

You know you've arrived when you see the sign which reads,

"How to survive in Death Valley". Furnace Creek is an oasis a few miles into the valley; though it is kept smart for the tourists it retains the uneasy atmosphere of a frontier town. I checked in at the only motel, then walked over to the saloon for a beer. A few horses were grazing in the shadows of the palm trees. It was evening but the temperature was still over one hundred. Inside the bar the juke-box was playing at full volume, above the racket the barmaid was shouting at a hunchbacked dwarf who was wearing a hearing-aid. He stared at me as I sat down. He looked hostile, as though he wanted to pick a fight.

"Don't take any notice of him," said the barmaid, "he's a mean bastard but he's too small to do anything about it."

In fact the dwarf seemed to hold the place together; everyone talked about him, pushed him, laughed at him and bought him drinks. Without him there would have been nothing to do except watch television. By nightfall all the men were drunk. A woman came in singing the words to "D-I-V-O-R-C-E". She was holding a raw steak to a black eye.

A man called out, "Hello, wife!" She took no notice but went to the juke box where she played every country & western hit over and over.

Later Anna Ratskin entered. She was alone. She saw me.

"Why, Mr Smolinsky," she said, "this is a coincidence."

I got her a beer.

"I suppose Mikel sent you to keep an eye on me," she said.

"He thinks you're having an affair," I said.

Anna Ratskin laughed. "No, Mr Smolinsky," she said, "I'm not having an affair. I'm leaving him because he sleeps with our daughter."

That took me by surprise.

"I see you don't believe me," she said, "but mark my words, Mikel is planning something big. Then he and Princess will disappear."

"Something to do with artichokes?" I said.

"Maybe," she said, "there have been trips to Castroville."

I didn't know who to believe any more.

"Listen, Mr Smolinsky," said Anna Ratskin, "I have lived with Mikel for twenty-eight years always doing what he wanted. I have gone along with all his schemes. But now he has gone too far. How can I remain his wife while he is fucking our daughter? I have had enough of compromises. I think I will be happier alone. I no longer need anyone with whom to share my feelings." She stood up.

We left the bar together. It was a beautiful night. The moon was full and the desert filled with reflections. I decided to take the short drive up to Zabriskie Point. At the sharp bend just below the Point I came across an old Mustang that had skidded off the road, a drunk from the bar was slumped over the wheel, the one who had called, "Hello, wife!" A Chevrolet pulled up alongside and the woman with the black eye got out.

"Thanks a million," she said to me, "but Momma can handle this."

"That's right," said the man, "Momma'll take care of me."

"I told you to come home with me," she said, "now look what you've gone and done."

"Sorry, Momma," said the man.

Such is family life in Death Valley.

I reckoned that Anna Ratskin was telling the truth but even so I decided to hang around Furnace Creek a while longer just to see if she met up with anyone. A couple of nights later I tailed her out to Zabriskie Point. I kept a long way behind, driving with my lights off. Someone was already there, waiting for her. They embraced. Had Mikel Ratskin been on the level after all? I left the car and crept toward where the couple was standing. The white rocks of Zabriskie Point glowed in the moonlight, making a scene so unearthly that it seemed as if a giant looking-glass were being held toward the moon. The moonlight also shone on the platinum hair of Anna's companion. This near the hair and the figure were unmistakable. What was Laura Lyle doing here? I crawled closer so that I could catch what they were saying.

"Mikel's been exploiting us both for years," Anna said. "I was his slave, you were his pimp. I raised Princess for him, now you've trained her to be good in bed. We can't let it go on."

"Mikel's always been kind to me," said Laura, "but you're right, what he's doing with Princess is disgusting."

"He'll pay for it," said Anna. "I intend to break his heart."

"How?" said Laura.

"By robbing him of the only thing he values," said Anna. "With your help I'm going to remove Princess from the scene."

"When?" said Laura. "Tomorrow night," said Anna, "bring her to the Palace. I'll arrange the rest."

I'd heard enough. Now I was in a hurry. But right on the bend at the bottom of the hill a Death Valley Fox was loping across the road. I braked but nothing happened, my foot went down to the floor, and the car swerved into the dunes. I was lucky, but the car was stuck like a beetle in a bathtub. So I hiked the rest of the way back to Furnace Creek.

I told the barmaid what had happened. "It's that frigging hunchback," she said, "if he doesn't like your face he'll fix your brakes."

It was dark when I finally got to Las Vegas. Ratskin was at the house.

"Where's Princess?" I called.

"With Laura," he said, "at the Palace."

Too late! "Listen carefully," I said, "there was no man. Anna was plotting with Laura to kidnap Princess."

Ratskin's look confirmed that Anna had been telling the truth.

"I suppose she told you about me and Princess," he said. "Well, you know what she looks like, Mr Smolinsky, can you blame me? Look, my shrink kept saying to me, 'If you're functioning okay with your repressions it's not worth the pain of getting rid of them.' But day by day Princess was getting more beautiful. And older. I began to dread the day when she would want to leave home. Finally I could stand it no longer. I told Laura. She arranged it all. Princess became my mistress. But now Laura is blackmailing me. So I decided on one final coup. I persuaded the farmers of Castroville to sell me their entire artichoke crop. I arranged for the hearts to be removed and replaced with nuggets of gold. Then I planned to export the whole lot to Israel. I intended to start a new life there. Just me and Princess." By the time he finished he was crying.

"Come on," I said, "we had better get to the Palace of the Princess."

Anna was already there. "Why, it's Mr Smolinsky," she said, "fancy seeing you again."

"Where's Princess?" hissed Ratskin.

"Won't you join me at my table," said Anna, "and we'll discuss the matter."

Ratskin had no choice. I stayed at the bar. The lights dimmed. Out came the Jackettes led by Laura Lyle; tonight they seemed even more manic, as if they were high before they began. There was something different about the mannequin too; tonight the female body looked all but animate as it lay crumpled in the corner waiting to be hacked to pieces. Then came a frenzy of movement as the Jackettes dragged the thing toward the centre of the stage. As the spotlight fell upon it I saw something that knocked me sideways, for around the mannequin's neck was a gold chain from which hung the word PRINCESS. I cried out but the noise of the bongos drowned my voice. Ratskin too had recognised the limp body on the stage. He was on his feet in an instant, but just as quick Anna pulled a gun and dared him to move. He was forced to watch helplessly as the Jackettes raved around the body of his daughter. So this was her revenge! I began to sprint toward the stage but I didn't get half-way there before a couple of Ratskin's gorillas grabbed me and thinking that I was a freak began twisting my arms. Meanwhile the Jackettes were approaching their climax, already several axes had bitten into the stage only inches from where Princess lay.

Suddenly there was a rush of air as every door was flung open and cops streamed in through the entrances.

"Don't anybody move!" they yelled.

Seeing her prize about to be snatched from her grasp Anna cracked. "Kill! Kill!" she screamed as she began to shoot wildly at the stage with her Saturday night special.

Immediately the cops opened fire on her, knocking her backwards over her own table. Panic-stricken the Jackettes fled in all directions. Only Princess remained on stage as the house lights went up, unconscious and naked. She was wrapped in a film of plastic that gave her skin an unnatural shiny look.

"Thank God you've come!" cried Ratskin as he ran toward his daughter.

"Hold your horses, Ratskin!" yelled the police chief, "I don't know what we interrupted here but we came for you. A matter of artichokes."

And Ratskin, already broken by his wife's plot, went quietly.

Virginia Lyle, getting wind of the circumstances, wrote to Princess offering her a job at the Institute of Oral Love. Laura tried to persuade her to accept. I argued against.

"But, Mr Smolinsky," said Princess, "who is going to look after me now Momma's dead and Poppa's in jail?"

"We'll find someone," I said.

"You don't understand, Mr Smolinsky," she said, "I'm three months pregnant. That's why Poppa and I were going to run away. I need a husband."

Being poor and having no family had not made me happy. Perhaps it was time to try being rich and married.

"Princess," I said, "will you be my wife?"

"Oh, Mr Smolinsky," said Princess, "you've got a heart of gold."